EX LIBRIS

VINTAGE CLASSICS

May 10 1845

Ah, Lord, isn't this great! A book full of empty pages and all of them for me. Today is my fourteenth birthday and my big brother Patrick gave me this to write in. "A way to keep hold of your thoughts, Phylly," he said. "To store up your secrets and dreams and build them into a world where you can roam freely wherever and whenever it takes your fancy."

Where to start? Oh, my name! Should I introduce myself to myself? Well, I will. Out of politeness and to give the pages a beginning. My name is Phyllis McCormack and those who love me, which is my family, call me Phylly. I live in Queen's County in the south of Ireland. We are Irish Catholics, and I can read and wri—

There's Ma calling! This is Phylly McCormack signing off. I have just realized that I haven't told a thing about myself or my life. Coming Ma! I'll begin with that tomorrow then.

May 11 1845

It's me again! I love this! I've been going about my day, helping with chores, my mind racing with the things I want to set down in my own private book!

Here's how we live. There's Ma and Da, then there's Pat, the eldest boy, and after him, me. Then, in age order, there's Hughie who's ten, Grace who is eight, Mikey's four and, lastly, baby Eileen who's six months. It's a struggle for space. We've just the one room and a covered bit out back where Ma and Da sleep. Still, we are blessed at our cottage because we have a bed, although we don't have covers for it. I have never visited one of those households where they have bedclothing. Irish linen and that kind of fancy stuff is produced up north and then shipped to England or France. Usually, it's bought by rich landowners. Most families here sleep on straw but, as I said, we have a bed.

What else? Oh, yes, we own a very greedy pig and a piglet. We feed them coarse potatoes – they're lumpier than the ones we grow for our own consuming. In the summer, when the pig has got nice and fat, Da takes it to market and sells it for cash. This money pays towards our rent. Da keeps a little

in reserve to make sure we can buy food, if we need to. For, by summer, our potato stock has run low and we have little to eat. Our lives are about scratching a living off the land.

My parents farm 16 acres, all of it rented. There are many who survive on less than five but those poor families are always close to starving, whatever season it is.

We are one of the few families in the neighbourhood who have a dog. He's called Mutt. He's black and wiry and a real mix of a fellow. I found him a year back running wild on the road, wounded, starving-thin and I begged Da to let me keep him. Da said yes, on condition that not one morsel of our food was spent on him and that, should things get bad again – meaning if there was another famine like the one in 1822, way before I was born – then I'd put him back out on the road to fend for himself. I agreed, but I never would. Next to Pat, I love Mutt best in all the world.

We also have a couple of chickens, which is another luxury. So, we are not so poor. In fact, we are better off than almost every family within walking distance of our crossroads. Our cottage is not insulated against the weather but we burn bog peat in the winter, which keeps us warm as toast. It gets awful smoky though because we don't have a chimney but, all in all, we are a happy band, us McCormacks. I have nothing to complain of. Except that I wish I was a boy!

May 12 1845

How is it that I can read and write and dozens of others, including Ma and Da, cannot? Well, in 1829, Daniel O'Connell – he's our national hero and I'll write more about him later – won back equal rights for Catholics. So now, we are entitled to go to school. I go to school and Pat went to school.

Pat says the pen is the purest weapon in the world. Da says Pat is a dreamer and nothing comes of dreams. But I'd follow him to the end of the world. Pat's dreaming makes the world shiny and bright. At school, I learn English and spelling. Mathematics too, but I'm not great with sums. Sometimes, if we are lucky, we learn geography. I love that best. I am always daydreaming about faraway places. I stare at the maps and picture myself travelling the whole world wide. I can point out France and England and the New World of America, which is bigger than both of the others stitched together. One day, I want to sail to America on one of those grand steamers I've seen in drawings. I shan't be afraid, even though I've never seen the sea.

There is another place on the map, big as America, but it's terrible far away. When we speak of it, it is with dread or sadness. It is a huge continent of a place called Australia and next to it is a smaller landmass, Van Diemen's Land. I don't ever want to go to those places for they are where the convicts are sent on the transportation ships.

May 13 1845

Ah, but this is grand! Having a diary of my own is like having a best friend who will never give my secrets away. But will I ever have any secrets that are *so* secret you grow breathless when you think them? This morning, when Pat and I were scything the grass, I asked him what sort of secrets he thought I should be filling these pages with. He threw back his head and laughed so loud I thought he'd crack open the blue sky overhead.

"You'll know them, Phylly, when you start thinking and feeling them. Trust me."

"So how should I fill the blank pages until they do occur to me?" I asked him.

"Write about yourself, and write about Ireland. Ireland as you see her and live her. Tell it through your eyes, Phylly."

"That's family and school and history," I said to Pat. "My diary will be boring then, because I'm no *seanchaí*!" *Seanchaí* is the Irish word for storyteller.

"Who knows, one day, you might be a real storyteller, little sister. Yes, I can see you as the red-haired, freckled *seanchaí* who travels the New World recounting tales of Ireland."

Later, I was thinking over what Pat had said and it seemed such a grand notion, to write about Ireland and travel the world with my tales. It would be the best dream in the world but I have no idea how I could ever achieve such a thing. What chance have I, an Irish country girl, of ever sailing the seas and visiting the New World of America? But I can begin with everything I see around me now. I shall write of what makes me happy and what makes me sad or afraid.

May 14 1845

I would never speak this thought but I can write it down. Though I adore Pat even more than Mutt, sometimes he makes me afraid. He argues all the time with Da. He is always talking politics and Da disapproves of politics. Da says, "Politics is dangerous and leads to dark crimes at night." Which it does in Ireland.

Pat attends "secret society" meetings, which are illegal. He, like many others in Ireland, wants to see an end to English rule here. He never says so but I think those "societies" plot against the British—

Oh, Lord, that's Ma calling me to the house to help with the feeding of Mikey, my youngest brother, and baby Eileen. It's a pity to go inside on such a warm evening, but I have to help. More later, if I can. If not, tomorrow.

May 15 1845

I was writing about what Da and Pat are always fighting over. Here in Ireland, Daniel O'Connell is known as "The Liberator" because he won back equal rights for Catholics and because he opposes the Act of Union which was made law by the British in 1800. This act abolished our Parliament in Dublin, leaving us to be governed by the British from Westminster. It is 45 years since we lost our government and there are many who are tired of British rule. They are fast losing faith in O'Connell. Pat is one of them.

May 17 1845

Yesterday evening, I asked Pat to tell me something about the secret societies so that I can write about their activities here.

"Don't write about them, Phylly," he said. "Write about the brave Young Irelanders."

"Tell me again about the Young Irelanders?" asks I, surprised, for I had not heard Pat speak too much about them.

"They are a fine young bunch of the most educated men, Phylly. They it is who have founded the daily newspaper, the *Nation*. . . Stop that laundering, Phylly, that's girl's chores. You come and sit yourself beside me on the grassy bank here and I'll tell you all about them." He patted the tufted earth beside him and I willingly laid the soap-suddy clothes to soak, wanting nothing better than to hear his tales.

May 20 1845

We've had no rain now for three weeks. It's glorious.

May 25 1845

I was so hot last night, I couldn't sleep. It's curious – so many warm days, one right after another. I like it better than the cold but it makes me lazy and I cannot think to write. I walk the fields in the evenings when I am not needed at the house. Sometimes, I take little Mikey with me and carry Eileen in my arms. We stay out for an hour or two to give Ma a break. We ford the river and splash our feet in the cool, clear water and search for fish. There are plenty of the silvery fellows darting to and fro.

June 3 1845

The grass is so dry, all straw-coloured and wilting. No one will ever again describe Ireland as the Emerald Isle if this heatwave continues!

June 17 1845

Ma and Da set off on their trip to Limerick. There's a grand market there. They go once a year to sell the pig who has grown deliciously fat and should fetch a good price. Our potato stock is beginning to get low so we'll be glad of the cash, and the supplies it'll buy us to get us through the summer. They'll be gone a few days so Pat and I took the four young 'uns swimming down at the river.

June 21 1845

The pig fetched a princely sum, said Da. It was great to have Ma and Da home again. I can rest for a bit now. Running a home, looking after babies is exhausting. I've not had a minute to write a word. When I am grown, I shan't have a family. I'll travel across America in a wagon meeting people and telling stories. Only if I'm homesick and lonely will I have babies!

July 12 1845

With some of the cash Ma and Da earnt selling the pig, Ma
sent Pat and me off to Roscrea. She wanted thread for a shift
she's sewing for little Eileen. She'd started it weeks ago but
could not go on with it until the pig had been sold and we'd
a bit of spare cash. It was a grand walk in the sunshine and
took us over an hour, passing by the river and then a leafy
walk all the way. When we reached the town there was a
grand crowd gathered in the main square. Drums, banners,
flags fluttering everywhere. The whole carry-on.

"Will you take a look at that!" cried Pat, pointing towards
the marchers.

"Keep quiet," says I, tugging him by the elbow, for I didn't
want him to get involved.

"We are all of us Irishmen, Phylly. Whether we be
Catholics or Protestants. Can't they see that?"

In Irish history the twelfth of July is known as the
Glorious Twelfth because it is the anniversary of the
Protestant victory over the Catholics at the Battle of the
Boyne. It upsets Pat to see them flagwaving and beating their
drums because he believes we should be working towards

creating a united Ireland, a republic, ruled by Irishmen whatever their religion.

It was market day in Roscrea. It's an age since I visited a market but even with a few pence in our pockets to spend there wasn't a lot of food on the stalls. These summer months are called the "meal months" because the only food available which is still edible is meal and even that is scarce. Prices rise high. Summer months are always tough because the new potato crop is not ready for harvesting until September and there's little else to eat.

All the time we were in the town and wandering round the market we could hear those drums rolling. I was glad when we were on the road to home again.

It is still glorious hot. This afternoon after we got back we went swimming again and I washed some clothes. A grand day – even if it is the Glorious Twelfth!

July 13 1845

Pat caught a salmon this afternoon! The size of the fellow! It was cause for great celebration. We cooked it in the yard on an open fire and ate it with relish.

As I sit writing the stars are shining bright. A young

neighbour, William, and his wife, Mary, have come by. William lives at the far end of our hamlet, up the lane about a mile and a half. He plays the fiddle, which is what he's doing now and our young 'uns are dancing to the music. My little sister, Grace, is wriggling and twisting like an earwig. How she loves to be the centre of attention! The crackling fire, the long evening and the merriment make my heart happy. Life is rich with blessings.

July 14 1845

A lively do in the yard again tonight. There was no salmon but plenty of dancing and *poteen*. Today is the anniversary of the French Revolution of 1789. It is an important date for us Irish because it inspired the birth of an organization called the Society of United Irishmen. Their main aim was to bring all the Irish together, both Catholic and Protestant, to create a single Republic of Ireland.

It is still gloriously hot. Nothing much to do outside on the land until the potato harvest. Dug up a few onions. Helped Ma with Eileen. Lazy, happy days.

I haven't been writing in my diary very much because I can't think what else to write about. I'll never make a storyteller!

July 26 1845

Ma's birthday. We sang and danced in the yard until way past bed-time. Ma looked radiant as Da took her by the hand and led her back and forth. Two families of neighbours joined us. They live up by the Ring of Elms. Even Father Timothy popped by to offer his blessings, and stayed for a sip (or three!) of *poteen*. He likes a drink, our parish priest does. *Poteen* is a home-made alcoholic brew. It's a bit like whiskey, made from grain and terrible strong! I would never drink it because I can't even stomach the smell of the stuff!

August 12 1845

There was a break in the weather this afternoon. Strange, after so many dry weeks. Sleet showers followed by thunder and lightning and then torrential rain. I stood at the door, staring out. "This could be the end of the world," I thought.

Mutt hid under the bed. I really laughed but Ma told me to throw the poor fella out. "Go wash the dishes and help with the supper!"

Even with all the young 'uns screaming and carrying on, I could hear him whining outside the door. But she wouldn't let me bring him in because he was so wet. It's not fair. Our pig was always inside. Still, thankfully, the pig has been sold and our rent paid. Lord, he was a smelly fat thing!

August 13 1845

Pat has a new friend called Ned. He came by today. I don't like him at all. He is dark and swarthy with mad staring eyes and doesn't say much. Leastways, not to any of us. Pat told me to be kind to him because both his parents were deported to Australia for stealing.

August 14 1845

It is much cooler since the rain. Da said this evening that he hopes this change in the weather won't affect our potato crops. He says he's had a feeling in his bones that we won't have a good harvest, but that's silly. He always worries. Every year, round harvest time, he starts grumbling.

"Why should a bit of rain make a difference?" I asked, but he just grunted and carried on eating. Patrick missed his meal. He would have got a right royal belting except that, when he finally arrived, he brought news that in the counties of Galway and Mayo the potato crops are "of the most luxuriant character". We all whooped and sung, even Da smiled. Oh, I like that word, luxuriant. It wraps itself around you like the promise of heaven!

August 20 1845

Da can stop worrying. The daily newspaper, The *Freeman's Journal* printed this today:

The growth of the potato plant progresses as favourably as the most sanguine farmer could wish.

I meant to find out what "sanguine" means but I had no chance, I've been so busy with the house. Sometimes, I wish I were the youngest girl instead of being the oldest. Why does being a girl mean that you get lumbered with the housework and looking after the babies? I am left with so little time to write in this diary. If I was a boy...

August 21 1845

Sanguine. I asked Pat what it means. He said, "Being of a hopeful disposition." So, even the most hopeful and expectant of all farmers could not wish for a better crop than the one we are about to harvest. What better news could there be?!

You see, we rely on the potato. It is simple to cook and cheap. And pigs, cattle and fowls can be reared on those that are too small for us to eat. Unless you are very rich, it is the main source of food.

Pat was in a very peculiar frame of mind this evening and went out straight after we'd eaten.

August 24 1845

Ned was here again this evening, the third time this week. I heard him whispering in the yard. He and Pat are up to no good, I'm sure of it, but I don't know what they are about. Still, it makes me cold with fear. I have to pretend I'm busy with chores so Ned doesn't suspect me of eavesdropping. When I watch Pat in his company, I see a change in my brother and it makes me concerned.

I know Pat is ardent about Irish liberty, but he doesn't have parents who have been transported by the British to the other side of the world so he has no reason to be hot-tempered. Why does he allow himself to get caught up in these matters? Even if we don't have political independence, our life is not so bad.

Da is right to refuse such talk in our house. "I'll not welcome any lad in this family spouting the words of an outlaw," he said during supper, glaring at Ned.

All this talk of revolution is creating a rift between Pat and Da and bad feelings in the house. Now Pat has started to stay away nights.

September 4 1845

I am worried. But I am nervous about writing anything that could get Pat into trouble. Suppose, one day, this diary fell into the wrong hands? Fortunately, Ma and Da cannot read so they will never learn of his activities through me or my writings. Not that I know what he's up to.

September 6 1845

Pat didn't come home. When he goes missing, I can't sleep. I wish he'd never met that Ned.

September 10 1845

Pat came looking for me at the river where I was washing the family's clothes. He looked troubled.

"What's up?" I cried, fearing he'd done something and got caught.

"There's bad talk of the crops, Phylly."

"What crops? Ours, you mean?" I was almost relieved not to hear news of guns and killing.

"Hard to say. Reports are differing everywhere. I hope for all our sakes, they'll be fine hereabouts."

"What have you heard?"

"In areas where the crop is good, the very next day potatoes dug from the selfsame ridges are black and rotten."

"Lord, no!"

"No one can explain it."

"Have you told Da?"

"Not yet."

"Well, we'll know soon enough about our own. He's starting up at the west ridge tomorrow. You'll be here to help, Pat, promise me? He's expecting it of you."

"Why wouldn't I be?" Pat answers me as though his

absences are in my imagination. Then his mood lifted when he talked of his meeting with some revolutionary friends. I love to hear what's happening in the country, but what he tells me frightens me.

And I hope Pat's wrong about the potatoes.

September 11 1845

Hell and damnation! See what the *Freeman's Journal* published today!

Disease in the Potato Crop

We regret to have to state that we have had communications from more than one well-informed correspondent announcing the fact of what is called "cholera" in potatoes in Ireland. In one instance the party had been digging potatoes – the finest he had ever seen – from a particular field, and a particular ridge of that field up to Monday last; and on digging in the same ridge on Tuesday he found the tubers all blasted, and unfit for the use of man or beast.

Pat says it's God's blessing that Ma and Da can't read. But the news will reach them soon enough. I bumped into Father Timothy up near the crossroads this morning. He was shaking his head, muttering like a madman and walking fast. "Phylly," he cried out when he saw me, "what has your Da to say of the news? I've visited three families this morning and they've sound potatoes, but there are some not so far from these parts who have found their crop blasted."

"We're only just beginning to dig, father," I replied.

"Pray, my girl," he muttered. "Pray for the Lord's blessing on Ireland and her crops." And he headed off in the direction of William and Mary's farm.

What if our crops prove to be disastrous? We will starve! I thought cholera was a disease that killed people, not vegetables!

September 14 1845

The potatoes from the west ridge are sound and scrumptious. Thank heavens we're not one of the areas affected, but God help those who are. Still, we have plenty more to dig yet. It's too early to feel easy.

September 16 1845

As our spades hit the earth, sinking into it, turning over the dark sods to reveal the crop, I close my eyes and pray. Each time I have opened them, I have gazed upon fat healthy potatoes. Thank you, Lord.

Some of our neighbours have not been so lucky. Da says we may have to share with the less fortunate. The talk is that many areas are blighted. But it's hard to know how far spread the blight is.

September 23 1845

Folk in Tipperary are turning out in their thousands to catch a glimpse of Daniel O'Connell who is touring there. Everyone waving green boughs and shouting: *"Welcome, ten thousand times welcome. . ."*

Bands have accompanied the processions, and groups representing the different trades. What a sight it must be.

Over 100,000 people outside Thurles. Wouldn't I love to have been amongst them at that Monster meeting!

One of the founders of the *Nation* newspaper, its editor Thomas Davis, has died.

September 27 1845

Pat told us all at supper that, two days ago, Robert Murray of the Provincial Bank of Ireland in Dublin wrote to Henry Goulburn, the Chancellor of the Exchequer in London, to say that the "alleged failure of the potato crop was very greatly exaggerated". Well, he should be here!

Do these smart businessmen walk about with their eyes closed? But, of course, when Mr Murray leaves the bank at night he goes home in a carriage and, no doubt, has a great deal more to eat than potatoes. So, even if there were none on his plate, he wouldn't notice the difference. What does this blight mean to the rich men and their families, I wonder? Funny, I've never thought about them before, about how different their lives must be compared to ours and how out of touch that must make them. Yet those government men, who know so little about us poor people, are making decisions that affect all our lives. I wonder, has Robert Murray ever been inside a cottier's home?

I would have voiced my opinion had I not noticed Da's expression. He looked heavy and pained and I knew he was worrying about how the country will feed itself through the coming year. I pray that the last of our crop to be dug up in a week or so will be sound. Still, though we may be one of the lucky families, even a partial blight will affect the whole nation because it will create food shortages.

September 28 1845

Sir Robert Peel, the Prime Minister of England and Ireland, has a funny nickname. When he was Chief Secretary for Ireland he made a habit of standing on his chair after dinner and, with one foot on the table, would drink a toast to the memory of William III, otherwise known as William of Orange. So Daniel O'Connell has christened Sir Robert "Orange Peel". I like that!

October 4 1845

Da, with the help of Hugh and Grace, dug up the last of the crop this morning and all our potatoes are sound. No sign of blight in any of them. There was a lot of hallooing and whooping, I can tell you. Now, we are storing them all in a dry pit to keep them cool and healthy throughout the coming months. The blight won't reach them there. Still, even with the whole crop safe and sound, it will be a short season and we'll all have to eat less and then think up ways to build up our meals. With the blight that's affected County Clare and numerous other areas, there'll be nothing left to buy next year. We had buttermilk with our meal tonight. It was a treat after nothing except water for the last month or two.

October 31 1845

"Orange Peel" called an emergency meeting of his Cabinet in London today. There's talk that he might abolish the

Corn Laws so that rice and corn can be freely imported into Ireland. The problem seems to be that many of his fellow ministers and his government are against such a move. I can't think why. Still, hurrah for "Orange Peel". And I thought he was the enemy. Not all English Protestants are ogres!

November 3 1845

O'Connell is trying to put an immediate stop to any kind of food being shipped out of Ireland and sold abroad. He is also insisting that everybody stop using grain to make *poteen*. The grains will be needed for food to eat, not for brewing alcohol. He has also requested the British to cancel the import taxes on food into Ireland. He wants us to be able to receive grain and Indian corn from the British colonies.

November 4 1845

Apparently, "Orange Peel" supports O'Connell in believing that all food produced in Ireland should stay in Ireland during this time of shortages. Unfortunately, his own government is not backing him. I hear they are tearing themselves into two sides over the issue. How could anybody oppose scrubbing out laws if those laws mean people can't be fed?

November 10 1845

Horrible! Horrible! The rot has destroyed most of the potatoes which were wholesome and sound when we dug them out of the ground. Da opened up the pit this morning and found it filled with nothing but diseased mush. All we have left to eat are those that hadn't yet gone underground.

"Six months' provisions are a mass of stinking rottenness. Where has it come from?" Da kept repeating all morning. "Disease will take us all," he drawled.

I felt my skin go cold when I heard him. What are we to do? We'll have to use the rent money to buy food, and then what? If we don't pay our rent, we will be thrown into the road.

December 1 1845

Five men, one of which was Ned, rapped on the door last evening asking for Da. They looked so serious, he stepped outside with them. I followed, saying I was after water to wash myself, and I hung about in the shadows trying to catch a phrase or two. There was a real exchange of words. All in whispers, until Da yelled, "Be on your way! And don't go bringing that kind of trouble on our heads. We'll not get involved, d'ya hear me?"

I was dying to know what they'd been discussing but when he came back in the house, he wouldn't say a thing about it. He kicked Mutt out from under his feet, which he never does unless he's moody as hell.

"If our Pat's involved in any of this," he said to Ma later when he thought we was all sleeping, "I'll turn him out and forbid him back. That kind will bring ruin on us all. Someone should soften the wool in that troublemaking fellow, Ned. The British won't stand for his carry on."

Ma told him not to get so het up. "You don't know that this has anything to do with Pat," she says. Then she begged him not to say a word when Pat got in, but Pat never came home. I hate it when he stays away. It only makes matters worse. What was the visit all about, I wonder?

December 3 1845

Winter's coming sharp. We've peat in plenty to keep warm but as to eating, I don't know how we are going to survive. We have some potatoes not blighted, but they won't be sufficient to last through to the next harvest. When they're gone, we will have nothing. There's talk of outbreaks of typhus fever in the workhouses. Apparently, it's a natural consequence of famine. *Famine.* I've rarely heard it mentioned in day-to-day speech before. Our teachers have mentioned it in history classes, but now it's on everyone's lips. Are we all going to starve?

December 4 1845

Ma's breastfeeding Eileen again. There's no milk there, she says. It's only so the poor little mite thinks she's getting fed. She doesn't understand that we'd feed her plenty if we could.

She's got horrid dark rings under her eyes, cries all the time and is thinner than Mutt. We kids all share the same bed so it means that when she starts yelling, even though she's in with Ma and Da, it stops all of us from sleeping. I'm so tired I've stopped doing my learning.

December 5 1845

"Orange Peel" has resigned! On account of Ireland and the battle over the Corn Laws. Fancy that! The opposition party is led by Lord John Russell. They are the Whigs and they will be the new government.

December 10 1845

I am beginning to understand why so many people believe that Ireland should be governed by the Irish. If Ireland was ruled by Ireland, we would be making decisions which were in the best interests of our own people. But, as I write these pages, tons of food are being exported from Ireland for sale abroad. Daniel O'Connell is demanding an end to all such exports. He insists that every mouthful stay here, to provide for the coming months when the potatoes that were not rotten have all been eaten up. Without potatoes, there will be precious little left to eat if every other food supply is exported. But still, in spite of what he advises, the ships are leaving from every Irish port laden with food: butter, eggs, oats, wheat, sheep, pigs. All of it for sale abroad.

I don't understand why we are exporting our produce when we do not have enough to eat. When I asked Pat, he said that it is to do with business. "It is about making money, Phylly, rather than caring for those individuals who are short of food. That is why we must fight for a self-governing Ireland," he says. He turns everything into politics. Perhaps he's right. I don't know.

December 14 1845

Eileen screams and hollers and drives us all crazy because she is not getting enough to eat. She cannot understand that we are all eating smaller portions. It's heart-scalding to hear her.

December 16 1845

My tummy rumbles all the time. Even when I've just finished my dinner! I'm getting thinner and I'm so tired.

December 20 1845

The *Nation* has quoted O'Connell as saying: "I will get all I can for Ireland and when I can I will take the rest."

December 24 1845

Pat came home this morning to spend Christmas with us. I was getting worried that he wouldn't be here. My parents were none too pleased with him. He's been gone for days, but he was light-hearted about his absence and told Da to stop worrying. "It's one less mouth to feed," he teased. It's great to have him here. There'll be stories aplenty round the fire even if there's not too much to fill our bellies.

December 25 1845

What a Christmas! Pat's tales of the goings and comings in London are keeping us all laughing and merry. Apparently, Queen Victoria sent for Lord John Russell, the Leader of the Whig Party, and invited him to form a government but, on account of this Corn Law business, he wasn't able to find enough support and was obliged to refuse her offer. This left her no choice but to inform old "Orange Peel" that she wouldn't accept his resignation. Now, he is back in power! Please God he is still intending to do something for Ireland. Even when we are not meaning to, we Irish are turning the British government on its head! Imagine Queen Victoria in a tizz not knowing from one minute to the next who is governing her country! Still, I bet she wasn't too troubled when it came to Christmas dinner. I bet she tucked in to a plate of plenty. A big fat hen or duck. Oh, wouldn't that be delicious!

January 3 1846

Oh, Lord, I'm so HAPPY! I've found a position at Errill Manor, the big house on whose estate we have our own smallholding. It's barely two miles' walk across fields to the south of here and I am to earn fourpence a day! Not a grand sum, but what a difference it will make to our lives. My duties are to wash floors and polish the silver and help out wherever I am needed. Scullerymaid, that is my title. Well, I'll be good at it. None better. I've been washing clothes for long enough.

The housekeeper took me into the kitchen – bigger than our entire cottage! – and there was all this food spread out on silver trays on the table. My eyes must have grown as large as saucers. I was mentally plotting how to shove some of it down the front of my shift when Mrs Murphy, that's the housekeeper (round as a penny she is), says to me: "And don't you go thinking that you can help yourself to anything in this house. If I spy light fingers, you're out. Remember, thieving lands you in the gaol." So I did a quick nod, thanking her for the job and sped off home. "And don't be even one minute late!" she called after me, but my feet had wings and I was halfway down the long driveway by then, and I didn't look back.

Wait till I tell Pat about the job. I bet, if I drew him a plan of the house, he could break in there at night while they're all sleeping, raid the kitchen and bring home the spoils for us all to gorge ourselves silly on. I couldn't begin to count how many rooms must be there. It's a palace, and so civilized.

January 4 1846

I was introduced to some of the other staff this morning. There's dozens of them. Gardeners, laundrymaids, cooks, stable boys, a dairymaid and butlers. What a business! I am by far the youngest but I don't care a fiddle. There's another maid, Mary, but she is much older than me. Nineteen, I'd guess, and as pretty as a picture with long auburn hair and big blue eyes. Her bones are as small as a bird and, alongside her, I feel a dumpy sight but she smiled and said Hello. So friendly she was, it took away my shyness. Mrs Murphy sits in the kitchen barking orders at us and smoking a clay *dudeen*. If I am anywhere near her when she's puffing, it sets my eyes watering. She scares me to death. I'm glad Ma doesn't smoke a pipe.

January 6 1846

There's a rack inside the front door up at the mansion. I was staring at it quizzically when a soft-hued voice behind me said, "It's to leave your shoes on when you enter from outside."

I turned, and there before me stood a young gentleman dressed in riding clothes. He must have been Pat's age, perhaps a wee bit older. I dropped my gaze and stared hard at my feet because I couldn't look. He was so handsome, his dark brown eyes were kind and... Oh, I am beginning to understand why Pat gave me these pages to write my secret thoughts in.

I wonder if he noticed that I don't have shoes. I've never owned stockings nor shoes in my life!

I nodded my thanks for his explanation and hurried off with my bucket clunking up the stairs. The corridors are long. I could get lost there for ever. When I opened several of the doors along the landing and peered inside I saw that they were all bedrooms. Six, seven, maybe even eight of them, and every single bedroom has a bed in it. Can you imagine that? More than that, there were linen sheets and pillowcases on the beds. I've never seen such elegance. And every bedroom has a fireplace with a chimney.

After I'd run off, I hid myself in one of the rooms while my heart was beating fast, inhaling the cleanness of it; laundry smells, dried petals in china bowls – they call it *pot pourri* – and polish on the wooden furniture. In the sweet stillness of it all, I tiptoed over to the window and leaned against the casement, gazing across field upon rolling field. The view goes on for ever!

In the gardens beneath where I was peering, there were flowers and leaves of every shape and size! Even now in winter, there was a grand variety of colours. I could never have dreamt that such tastefulness and luxury existed. And, in amongst it all, lives the young man with the dark eyes.

It's like waking up from a dead-of-night sleep and finding yourself in a world of fairy tales where the sky glistens brightly and the birds sing sweetly. I pinch myself but the house is real and I have the right to be there and a hot bowl of soup every lunchtime!

January 10 1846

The young man who is as handsome as a prince is called Edward! I passed him in the corridor near the scullery – Lord knows what he was doing in that part of the building – and he says to me, "Hello again."

I bobbed a sort of clumsy curtsey because I didn't know what else to do and because I was flabbergasted that he recognized me. Then he held out his hand to me, eyes warm and sparkling, and said, "Don't curtsey. Just tell me your name."

"Phylly's my name," says I, and I grabbed a hold of my scrubbing brush and beat a hasty retreat. Out of fright, not because I *wanted* to leave.

Mrs Murphy says he is the only son of the house, I heard her gossiping. (I wouldn't have asked. I couldn't mention his name. I couldn't share a dream that's as shiny as a shilling and have her laugh at me or scold me for my nonsense.) So, all my learning and studying means something, just as Pat promised it one day would. It means I can converse with Edward if I bump into him again and if he speaks to me some more.

Edward. No name was ever sweeter!

January 15 1846

They have a library up at the house. Fancy such a thing! A library in your own house! I haven't let on that I can read and write. Do all rich families have libraries in their homes? I'll ask Pat when I see him again, though he has not been back for a couple of days.

I saw Mary, the kitchenmaid, slip a bar of soap under her shift this afternoon. I tried to creep off so she wouldn't know as how I'd been there but she turned round sharpish and saw me.

"Phylly!" she whispered, but forcefully. I had no choice but to hear her.

"What is it?"

"You'll not say a word!" Her cheeks were flushed with guilt or fear.

"I don't know what you're talking about," says I and went off about my business. I know it's a sin to tell a lie but, God forgive me, my family cannot afford for me to lose this job and anyway I don't want to turn on Mary, one against another. If Mrs Murphy catches her, then that's their affair. I shall play innocent, for innocent I am.

February 2 1846

Mutt's sick. He's so thin and Da says we can't feed him any more. There's nothing to spare. Everything we have, we must keep to feed us. I watched Mutt lying all afternoon under the big tree at the turn in the lane. He looked so weak I thought he'd never get up again. I crept there when no one was about and gave him the dry bread I'd rummaged from out of the leavings in the bin up at the manor. He licked my face and then lay down again. Normally, he would have followed me. I HATE this situation!

February 5 1846

The words go out of shape as I write them due to damp blotches on the page. Eileen passed away this morning. I was just leaving for work when she breathed her last. It was horrible. Still, I had to go. We have to eat. Have food on our table. I was battling all day against my feelings. Being as how I am the beginner, I had to show a bit of brightness but it nearly broke my scalding heart to do it. I was glad of the work though, to take my mind off the loss of my baby sister. I scrubbed floors with such vengeance that Mrs Murphy admitted they'd never been shinier.

February 6 1846

Pat's been staying out all night again. Da was furious with him when he rolled up this evening but I think Da's anger was to cover his upset about Eileen. I've never seen my father with glistening eyes before. I was furious with Pat too, but only because I wish he'd take me with him. When we were on our own outside in the yard, he whispered, "Eileen is the last straw."

"What do you mean?"

"You know what I mean, Phylly." His blue eyes were burning, but after all he's been telling me, I had a sneaky suspicion I knew what he was going to say. "Ireland must cut all ties with England. And if the British will not agree to give Ireland back, then we will have to do whatever we must to win our country back."

I'm scared of what Pat means by such talk, of what he might do. Why can't he see things Ma's way sometimes? "It's God's will, Phylly," she says. "He has taken little Eileen to be with Him and the angels in heaven and we must be glad for her. She's to be spared the hardship of the summer ahead, and that must be a blessing."

Pat said Ma talks empty and Da's response was: "I'll thank you to keep your troublemaking opinions to yerself, young man, or be away from here!" So Pat, in fury, stormed out, slamming the door behind him. Again.

I lay listening to the others breathing and wheezing in the room while I was trying to sleep. I felt a dampness on my face and realized it was my own tears.

February 7 1846

Eileen's funeral. Mrs Murphy let me come in late, so I could be there. It was only us and Father Timothy, who said prayers. The rain made it bleaker.

After it was over, I trudged across the drenched fields to work. When I arrived I was shivering and Mary offered to fetch me a blanket but I said I didn't want no fuss. She's nice. I'd hate to see her land in gaol for the soap she filched.

I passed the dark-eyed young man on the stairs today. He is so different to anyone I ever met before. Such an educated gentleman. I heard Mrs Murphy say to him: "Master Edward, sir." Fancy that, someone addressing you like that in your own house. I would have liked to say hello, but my eyes were red and puffy, and I was too shy. He didn't seem to remember that he'd spoken to me the other day. I wonder why he's always on his own.

Ma was sneezing and coughing this evening. She must have caught it this morning when we were standing in the rain. Poor little Eileen. It's hard to comprehend it.

February 8 1846

Father Timothy was at our cottage when I got back. Ma'd been crying and he was talking to her, in whispers. When they saw me, they pretended everything was normal. But how could it be normal? When I was stoking the fire, he asked me had I seen Pat and I shook my head. "No good'll come to that brother of yours with his foolish talk and the company he keeps," he pronounced sternly. As he went on his way, he said, "*Dia Linn*" which means "God be with us" in Irish. It's going to take a miracle to save us all now.

February 10 1846

Pat's stir crazy. He's cold and angry and it breaks my heart. "O'Connell's not doing enough. Since the English threw the poor fellow in prison a year and more back, he's gone soft," so says Pat.

"Why?" I asked him.

"Because he agrees that Ireland should be given the right to govern herself but he thinks we should remain a British territory. That's a compromise. This struggle has gone on too long. We are close to starving while our food is sold abroad. Would that happen if we controlled our own fate?"

Such anger will surely lead him to harm. In any case, he blames O'Connell too quickly. It was O'Connell, before Christmas, who drew attention to all the food leaving Ireland. Even Peel has battled with his own government to do away with the Corn Laws.

February 11 1846

Only the potatoes are blighted. All our other produce is succulent and delicious, but it's being exported! I don't understand. Politics and economics leave me confused. Neither seem to have the interests of the people at heart. Even those Irish who are not so fussed about being self-governing are fussed about going hungry while others abroad make profits out of our food. If anything will cause uprisings then this might.

February 14 1846

The day before yesterday one of the great Irish landowners, a Marquess someone-or-other, declared in the House of Lords that many parts of Ireland are already in a state of revolt. He demanded police protection for landlords. Pat says it is going to get tougher. As people get hungrier, the violence will increase and the law will clamp down even harder against the poor people.

February 16 1846

When I dusted the hallway today, I peeped into the library and there was Edward, head buried in a book. I longed to go in. His dark hair was falling over his fingers pressed against his face. Very studious, he is. And kind-featured. I wonder what he reads all the days.

February 24 1846

I heard talk today that there have been outbreaks of unruly behaviour – not here in Queen's County – but elsewhere where the food shortages are acute. The English government is passing a new law which will help keep control should the troubles or protests get any worse.

February 25 1846

A strict curfew is being introduced. I didn't understand the word curfew so I blurted out the question in the kitchen up at the big house. Everyone glanced nervously at one another as though I'd said something embarrassing. This puzzled me.

"What's up?" I asked.

"Best not to talk on these matters," said Mrs Murphy, "not even in the privacy of this room."

"Why not?" I insisted.

"That's enough now," she chided, and then she changed the subject by sending everyone about their chores without them having finished their soup.

But later Gerard – he's the head gardener and a kindly soul who takes an age to tell a tale because he stutters – called me aside in the yard later and explained it to me. "A curfew," he stammered, "is a rule which limits people's movement."

"I don't understand, Gerard."

"Look at it this way. Between sunset and sunrise, nobody is allowed to leave their homes. If they do, they will be arrested."

Arrested, how frightening! After work, I raced across the

fields scared out of my wits that the sun might set before I was in the door!

Da was saying this evening that it is now a criminal offence to possess any type of weapon. A magistrate has the power to sentence anyone suspected of owning, carrying or stealing firearms to TRANSPORTATION for SEVEN YEARS!

I couldn't sleep this night imagining Pat breaking the curfew or carrying weapons or plotting some sort of a rebellion. Sooner or later he'll get caught.

February 26 1846

I'm scared, or my imagination is working overtime. I feel as though plots are being hatched everywhere! Even up at the great house. I was passing the stables this morning, on my way to empty the pails, when I spied Hugh and Dominic, two of the grooms, whispering deep into each other's collars. As soon as they set eyes on me they made as though they weren't talking at all and went on brushing the horses. They behaved as though I was the enemy! Even Mrs Murphy has gone funny. Her face was flushed bright fuchsia this morning. I think she'd been at the *poteen* last night! She has a sister from Lismany who died last week from fever.

February 28 1846

It's shocking cold these mornings when I wake. The water in the pails is iced over so I hate to wash, but I know I must.

The potatoes we are cooking at home are not wholesome. Ma says if they are boiled, then squeezed in a cloth and made into *boxty*, that's potato cakes, they'll be fine. But they're disgusting. I had gut-ache all day from eating the blasted things.

Mrs Murphy says she's going to ask if all servants can be given a hunk of bread with our bowl of soup. What a blessing that would be! One less mouth to feed at home. Da says he wants to save my earnings for the months to come. He says victuals will be hard to come by soon, even at crippling prices. If everything hasn't been sold abroad, that is!

March 1 1846

Something terrible's happened! And Pat's involved. This morning, when I was about ready to set off for work, two men from the constabulary arrived at our cottage, banging at our door, frightening the wits out of us all and demanding to talk with Pat. Da told them that we'd seen no sign of him for two days. That response is sure to go against Pat because one of the two, a short beady-eyed fellow, jumped down Da's throat: "So, you couldn't vouchsafe for his presence here in the house the night before last then?"

Da sensed the gravity of the situation instantly. He screwed up his face, frowning and asked: "If it's my eldest son you're looking for, you'll do me the honour of telling me what it is you're wanting to see him about?"

"Your boy, Patrick McCormack, has got himself mixed up with trouble. And he's to be arrested for possession of arms and assaulting other people's habitation."

Ma, when she heard this, clutched her stomach as though she were ailing and began to cry.

"Hush, woman!" says Da, too sharp, I thought, considering she's still suffering the loss of little Eileen. "Let's hear it, then," he says.

And the policeman recounted the whole of the episode which had taken place. (I couldn't believe all that I was hearing, but I never doubted the truth of it. In my heart I knew Pat's words would one day turn to action.) "Six men, all of them with their faces covered, marched on William Henderson's house..."

"And who might William Henderson be? He's not from round these parts, that's for sure."

"Henderson is a landlord of some repute. His estate is situated on the northerly reaches of Tipperary."

"And what about him?" Da was in a right royal mood.

"It appears Henderson turned a family out of their cottage a few weeks back for failing to pay their rent. No doubt he wanted the cottage for another bunch who had agreed to give him a higher rent or he had settled on some arrangement which was better to his advantage."

"You know as well as I do, promising to pay a higher rent and actually finding the money to pay it," butts in Da on the defensive, "are two quite separate affairs and the man's a fool, mighty landlord or not, to believe that the money can be found. Particularly in these times with famine waiting round the next corner—"

"Nonetheless, it doesn't call for cloak of darkness responses. Ribbonism, or any form of secret activity – even the gathering of groups of men to pin threatening notices to doors – or forcibly entering another man's home, all to arms, are illegal acts.

The six men waited until the dead of night and then entered through a gate in the garden and broke the back door down to gain entry to the house. Nobody was harmed but they threatened the landlord who they'd disturbed in his bed, warning him that *his life would be in danger* if any more of his tenants were evicted or troubled due to late payments. If convicted, your boy could be deported for this."

"You'll have to find him first," snaps Da, "and if you do, you'll have seen a great deal more of him than we have." And with that he slammed the door shut.

The mood was black in the house, and I was late for work. But I couldn't make myself move. Pat deported! Such a threat made my head swirl sickly.

March 2 1846

The famine is spreading. Even those counties that were not hit by the potato blight are running low on food supplies now. I am so lucky to have found employment. There's a bit of money coming in and I have soup to eat.

March 4 1846

Life's no fun without Pat. It's days since he's been here. He must be in hiding somewhere. I miss him achingly and wish he'd sneak back to steal me away with him. Da says, "He'll never set foot in this house again," but how can he say such a hateful thing when Pat's only caring for our rights? Still, I wish he'd concern himself with feeding everyone and forget Repeal for the time being. Does it make a difference who rules a country when the population is hungry? Besides, I have no one to go fishing with and it's too perishing cold for swimming.

March 6 1846

I am scared out of my wits for Pat. I wish he'd make contact, let us know that he is all right. If he were transported, would we be told about it? Where would he be sent? Will we ever see him again? I wish Da would not stay so angry with him, forbidding him here unless he gives up his ways. Then he could come home.

I learnt today from Mary that Edward is an only child and his ma died when he was a boy.

Mary has a small baby, a little girl named Lucy. I didn't ask her where the father is or if that's why she steals. She took a loaf while we were on our own in the kitchen. I watched her bury it in amongst a basket of laundry, ready for collecting as she left for home. She must've known I could see what she was up to, though I pretended not to notice because I don't want to be involved. It's way too risky.

March 9 1846

Spring will soon be here and my heart is lighter. A wave of hopefulness is sweeping over Ireland and the Irish people. Word is spreading in all parts that the British have established a Relief Commission. Apparently, it was set up late last year. Food is to be brought into the country. As I write, there are boats loaded with Indian corn on their way from America. In some parts of Ireland the rations have already arrived and are being stored in depots waiting to fight the famine. So, the English government is going to do something for Ireland at last. I had doubted their ability to care. I judged them by history which is why I had so little faith. Still, history does not always repeat itself. The British government, under instruction from dear old "Orange Peel", is going to issue food to the whole population and we will none of us go hungry!

Please God, when Pat hears this, he will hurry home. Please God, he is safe and has not got himself into trouble with his anti-British activities. Da was right. Pat has been led on a wild and dangerous path by the likes of troublemakers such as Ned.

March 10 1846

This afternoon Mrs Murphy quizzed me about the silver. She asked if I had misplaced one of the best silver spoons. "You cleaned both sets this week, did you not?" I nodded. Then she wanted to know had I counted the spoons and, if so, how many there had been. I couldn't for the life of me recall.

"The usual dozen, I suppose," I said.

She fixed me such a gaze. "Daydreaming will have you out of a job, my girl. It's your weakness, Phyllis McCormack, and don't say it's not because I keep my eye on you. If a spoon's missing, that's your responsibility." Lord, does she think I filched it?

One bit of good news. She told me it has been agreed, I suppose with the owner of Errill Manor – that's Edward's father who lives in England – that each member of the staff is to be entitled to a large hunk of bread with their soup at midday. So, she's not always a dragon!

March 12 1846

The silver spoon turned up. It was put away with the wrong set. I got the blame for it. I said nothing but sure as I'm writing here now, I don't remember muddling up the services.

March 13 1846

They are saying up at the manor that the need for food is growing urgent and making some desperate. What has happened to the corn that was on its way?

Mrs Murphy barks less since her sister died. I think she is grieving. Just like Ma is over Eileen.

March 14 1846

This morning, while washing the floor in the library, I crept over to one of the bookshelves and ran my fingers along the spines of the books. I wanted to feel their texture. Rows and rows of them. Some were bound in old scuffed leather with faded letters spelling words in languages I don't understand, and even in alphabets I've never set eyes on before. I slid one book from its place and opened it. It smelt fine and the paper was as delicate as silk. Poetry, I think it must have been, for the lines were shorter and more regular than in ordinary writing. It was written by a person called Jean Bapiste Racine. I stood turning over the pages wondering what it might be about when, suddenly, the door opened and Edward walked in. I nearly jumped out of my skin. I pretended to dust the cover and, as soon as I could, I stuffed it back on to the shelf. Edward seemed preoccupied and didn't even notice. Just as well because he must know that scullerymaids don't do dusting. That's Mary's work.

I grabbed my pail and made to go. It was only the noise of me moving, I think, that woke him up to the fact that there was anyone else in the room. "Oh, hello, Phylly. Please, don't leave. Go on with whatever you were doing and ignore me."

Ignore him! How could I? My heart beats wildly every time I glimpse him. And the thrill when he mentions my name!

"Yes, sir," I replied, calm as I could.

I must have begun to hum as I scrubbed, without even realizing I was doing it, because suddenly he asked, "Do you like to sing, Phylly? I wonder what makes you so happy."

I stood there stupidly not knowing what to reply. Finally, I mumbled something about "Orange Peel" and his food relief. It seemed an intelligent answer to give to a scholarly young man and I would hate Edward to judge me a fool with nothing but pails and soapsuds in my head. In any case, I could hardly admit that it was being near him that made my heart tralala and my lips just follow on. He laid down his pen and looked hard at me. "Well, if you are interested, then let us discuss it."

"Discuss what?" says I, having already forgotten what response I'd given him.

"The flaw in Peel's relief plan."

"Is there one?" I retorted, wishing Pat were close because he would have known what to say and he could have schooled me in it.

"Indeed, there is. The Prime Minister doesn't seem to understand that the great majority of Irish people never buy food. They grow potatoes and they eat what they grow."

I stared at the duster in my hand. How is it that I can discuss with Pat for hours on end and yet here I couldn't think of a single thing to say?

"Don't you agree, Phylly?"

"My family lives on potatoes," I stammered, babbling nervously, words tumbling from my lips. "There's no shame in it! In most Irish homes potatoes are the diet, and water or buttermilk the drink. We grow oats to sell and we fatten a pig for market but all that money goes directly to our landlord. . ." I had got so flushed and carried away that I had completely forgotten that I was standing face to face with the landlord's son who was smiling broadly at me. Or was he laughing? "Excuse me, sir, I best be going. Mrs Murphy'll be looking for me."

I made for the door and as I went, I passed my gaze over the vast array of books, shelf upon shelf of bound editions, an unknown world to me, and Edward at his desk in the centre of it all. I sighed, feeling foolish and ignorant. How I longed to share all the stories and languages with him.

"Phylly?"

"Yes?"

"Do you go to school?"

"I have been, sir."

"And do you read?"

I nodded. "But I haven't touched none of the books, sir," I added sharpish, remembering Mary and her filching of the soap and loaf and the missing spoon which had turned up.

"Please feel free to come in here and read whenever you want to. When Mrs Murphy doesn't need you, that is. I have no desire to distract you from your work."

I was confused. I didn't know what to say. I nodded my thanks and disappeared. We've never had books in our home. Books are for schooling. I was curious about what Edward was doing in there every day. Is he writing up the land accounts? Or is he studying?

March 16 1846

It is now six months since blight struck the potatoes. In some areas people are beginning to die. Black Fever and now another sickness they're calling Yellow Fever, on account of it turning the skin all yellow, are being contracted from north to south and from east to west, by poor starving folk eating potatoes that are diseased. Not five minutes beyond our own hamlet, up by the Ring of Elms near the wooden cross, I passed a family of beggars yesterday. They're the first I've seen, though the manor staff are saying that whole families are lying down in fields and roadsides and dying from sickness and lack of food. It seems a lifetime away till autumn when the new crop will be harvested and we can begin to eat and live again.

March 17 1846

St Patrick's day. None of the usual celebrating.

March 19 1846

They are setting up fever hospitals. The Famine Fever – that's the name everyone is giving to the Black and Yellow Fevers – is breaking out across the land. Typhus, some call it. Dysentery is everywhere too. The Commissioners cannot find enough nursing staff. The hope of just a few days ago has turned bleak. The people are so desperate there's news of riots in some towns. Why aren't they distributing the Indian corn we've been promised?

March 20 1846

The numbers of dead are rising. Hunger and disease and the squalid conditions for the homeless are the root causes. Even some of the nuns and doctors who are nursing the sick are catching the sicknesses and dying off. And what is England doing about it all? Precious little, as far as I can see. So much for the Act of Union. We are only a part of Britain when it suits them. They can take from Ireland whatever they fancy, but when it comes to helping out, that's another story!

I am beginning to understand Pat's anger. How I miss him! If I could only hear from him and know that he is safe.

March 21 1846

I can barely bring myself to write the news that we are hearing. Up at the manor, the gossip in the kitchen is of people being thrown out of their homes. The potato failure of last year has meant that hundreds of families cannot pay their rents. According to Gerard, 300 tenants in County Galway were evicted a week back. They were not squatters or paupers living in mud huts neither. They are folk of good standing and the landlords threw them out with the help of the police and military troops. Now the landlords can use the land for grazing their own beasts!

Here's what happened (according to Gerard): The inhabitants in the village of Ballinglass in County Galway were not in arrears with their rent. They had their houses built solid and in good order – there were no reasons for their landlords to complain. They had even worked hard to reclaim about 400 acres of land from a nearby bog. Still, early one morning last week, without any warning, into the village arrives a detachment of infantry, led by their commanding captain, as well as numerous police officers and a Sheriff with his men. There and then, tenants were called upon to give up their homes, which understandably they refused to do. The Sheriff spoke out saying it was an official call and that they – 61 houses in all – were to relinquish possession instantly.

Then, without further ado, the troops began to demolish the homes of these citizens. They tore off the roofs, ripped away walls. Women were crying, running here and there, clutching their babes tight in their arms. Youngsters were grabbing hold of bits of buildings, pinning themselves up against door frames trying to stop any further destruction, but all to no use. They were forcibly thrust away and flung to the ground. People were screaming and hurrying about with bits of property clutched against their breasts and belongings held tight for fear that they were to be robbed of every last thing. The troops – many were Irishmen – paid no heed even when others cursed them for their wrongdoings.

By the following day the entire village had been razed to the ground. Not a stick of a home was left. The people had been run out and left with nowhere to sleep except the ditches by the roadsides. The foundations of the houses were dug up and no one was allowed to bed down anywhere near them.

March 22 1846

As I was leaving today Mrs Murphy came into the kitchen and took me by the arm. She looked so stern I thought I'd done something wrong. "Put this inside your shift and take it home to your family," she said, waddling over to the larder and pulling out a chicken. A whole cooked chicken! I couldn't believe my eyes and I stood there like a lump as though I'd no arms to accept it with. "Go on, girl," she said. "Take it. I'm no revolutionary, don't know one group from the next, but I know injustice when I hear it. And what Gerard told us yesterday has quite shaken me. We peasant-folk must look after one another now, is my reckoning."

I never heard her talk like that before, or give away food from the Manor. I thought she must have been tippling the whiskey in the drawing room!

"What news of that brother of yours?" she asked as I was hastening out the door, loaded down with supper.

"No news," I answered, running off before she changed her mind.

At home, after our prayers, we made a right royal meal of the fowl. We are six now, without little Eileen and with Pat disappeared. We ate greedily, until hunger was gone, but the mood was not gay, not like it would have been a year back. There were no songs sung, no fireside stories told. Storytelling always used to be a favourite pastime in our house. I loved the romantic and heroic tales the best, those with giants and kings and fairies striding the earth, battling with witches and evil spirits, putting all to rights. Oh, that the magic of those legends could put all to rights now!

Ma was crying as she blew out the candle. She thought none of us was looking but I saw her and, as I lay my head down to sleep, I felt helpless. She must be fearing for our future, too.

March 23 1846

I was polishing silver in the kitchen this morning, trying to keep awake. I couldn't sleep last night worrying if Edward's family are going to turn us out of our home. Where would we go? How would Pat ever find us?

I would never have dreamt that the failure of one season's crop of stupid potatoes could cause such upset. Steaming with these thoughts, hardly aware of what I was doing, I set down the half-polished jug and went marching off in search of Edward. He was in the library, as usual, but instead of feeling tongue-tied, I peered round the door and requested a word. He looked surprised, but agreed and laid down his pen while those big brown eyes of his watched me approach. I was too raw for my stomach to turn over as it usually does when I see him.

"Edward, if you are my friend. . ." I began. What a nerve, for he has never made a declaration of friendship! ". . .and if our conversations have meant anything at all to you, if you care for Ireland or for any of us living in it, I beg you, talk to your father. . ."

My courage was up and my cheeks burning. On I went,

standing stiff as starch, hell bent on saying everything before I was thrown out on my ear.

"My da's not behind on our rent. Not so far, and we still have a baby pig to sell even though it's not as plump as before Christmas and we'd have been better off selling it then, but all is not lost, so we are luckier than many. . ." A deep breath, and I continued. "Please, beg your father not to be cruel with us, nor the families living up by the crossroads and near the church or wooden cross. You have plenty, clothes on your beds and food abounding in the larder. Don't turn us out. My little sister's in heaven already and my dog, Mutt, is all but dead. Others have suffered worse, I know, but it's no excuse for injustice. If you and your family set a good example, if people can see that not all wealthy landlords are cruel, who knows, things might change. The hate and the fear might stop and—"

"Whoa, Phylly, whoa," he replied softly and rose from his chair. "Firstly, I don't have the power to do as you request—"

"You do!" I cried. "Don't blarney with me, I beseech you."

"Sit down, Phylly. Let me explain. Then, you will see that my family haven't the power you believe us to possess."

I was baffled. My heart was telling me that Edward wouldn't lie to me – somewhere, within the meeting of our eyes, we had become deep, our souls were bonding, even if our day-to-day lives were far apart. Yet now, as he drew up a chair and led me to it, my head was spinning and the words of Pat and his dark friend, Ned, came flooding into my brain. They were warning me that I was making a ghastly mistake. To trust a wealthy landowner's son, what kind of foolish girl was I? I had been seduced by a gentle manner and the twinkling sweetness of his voice (for when he speaks, it is with a soft Irish lilt).

"Let me go!" I retorted and made to rise. "You've 5,000 acres and more!"

"Phylly, please."

His smile won the round and I remained where I was.

"Explain it to me, then," I said, "but don't take me for a fool."

"It's a complicated business, Phylly. So don't lose your patience with me. Keep your wildness still for a while. I am your friend and proud to be. So trust me."

"Tell me, then, and I'll be patient."

"My father is what is known as an absentee landlord because he doesn't live here. Like many such men, he doesn't want the responsibility of travelling back and forth from London, twelve hours each way on the boat, to collect his rents. So, a few years back, he leased our entire estate to one man who divided the land up into dozens of smallholdings. Each of these plots is rented out to a family like yours who pays heavily for their few acres. That middle man gets rich and my father gets paid on time. Are you following the gist?"

I nodded slowly, trying to understand what Edward was telling me. I hadn't ever considered that we might not be his tenants. Did Da know?

"So who should I be begging then," I asked, "if you truly have no power to help us? Could you not talk to your middle man on our behalf? You can't know the fear that has set in at home."

"It's true, Phylly, I cannot know it. But I am an Irishman. I can see what's eating into the system here and it makes me ashamed. . ."

I stared hard at him.

"Your eyes, your expression tell me that you don't believe me."

"What lies are you telling me? You are English. Not five minutes ago, you admitted that your da is English."

"But I was born here in Queen's County. This is my country. My father wants me to go to university in England but I have my heart set on Dublin. I may be a Protestant, Phylly, but, Protestant or Catholic, we are both Irish. I want to read law at Trinity and follow in the footsteps of Daniel O'Connell and—"

"He and we's Catholics," I snapped, for I was confused, surprised and thrilled all at once. "Oh, Lord. . ." I bowed my head because I felt foolish for getting so irate.

"What's wrong?"

"I sound like my brother . . . wherever he is," I whispered.

70

"Is your brother gone and fighting?"

"I couldn't rightly tell you," I lied. I recalled sitting on the riverbank the day Pat spoke to me of the Young Irelanders, and my heart yearned for that brother of mine. "If I trusted you and told you of Pat, how do I know that you wouldn't report him to the constabulary and have him shipped out on one of those great steamers to Australia?"

"Is that what you think I'd do?"

"No, because even if I knew his whereabouts, I'd never let on!"

Edward regarded me thoughtfully. Decision made, he hurried to the bay window, fetched a set of wooden steps and rested it up against a wall of books. He climbed to the highest rung and, after a glance in my direction, lifted two books out from the top shelf. He signalled to me to come and take them from him, which I did. I waited at the foot of the ladder, gazing up at his elevated frame, while he busied himself in the space where the books had been. Slowly, a fist clutched tight, he descended, hurried to the door and turned the key.

My stomach flipped like a seal on a rock. I was trembling happily, but what would Mrs Murphy say if she discovered me locked in here with the young master?

"Put the books on the table, then come over here and close your eyes, please." I did as he requested, squeezing my lids tight, dreaming of Edward kissing me.

"Hold out your hand."

Again, I did as I'd been bidden. Something like a square piece of cardboard settled in my work-soiled palm.

"Open your eyes."

I stared curiously. What I was holding was a green card.

"Has your brother shown you one of these, Phylly?"

I shook my head.

"You see what it says, Phylly? Catholic and Protestant must bond together as Irish citizens. My father may be of English blood but I'm Irish-born and no different to you or your brother."

I lifted my gaze to search into him, to understand what he was telling me.

"I'm with you, Phylly. And more. I'm standing with the Young Irelanders behind Thomas Francis Meagher, William Smith O'Brien, Gavan Duffy and the rest of them."

I was dumbfounded.

Suddenly, the handle on the door began to turn and rattle. It was followed by a knock. The intrusion caught us unawares and I nearly jumped out of my skin. Edward grabbed the card from me and shoved it into his pocket. "Who is it?" he called as he hurried to the table, picked up the books and scaled the steps.

"Sorry to have disturbed you, Master Edward, sir. I was thinking young Phyllis might have been cleaning the floors. I'd no notion you were in there. Begging your pardon, sir."

"One second." His manner was calm, reassuring and kindly. As he spoke he signalled me to move across the room out of sight, which I did, tiptoeing fast, trying not to let the soles of my bare feet squeak against the polished wooden floor. Edward crossed to the door and unlocked it. "Can I help, Mrs Murphy?"

"No, sir. Awful sorry to have troubled you at your work." And with that she was gone. I heaved a great sigh. Edward closed the door and turned back to me. His eyes were laughing mischievously.

"I must get back, before I lose my job." I began to move. My mind was all at sixes and sevens. Edward had not offered me the reassurance I sought for my family and our cottage but he *had* confided in me. I would never in my wildest moments have dreamt of such a possibility.

"The Young Ireland movement is our hope, Phylly. We – you and I and your brother and all the others – we will be this country's future. A free independent Ireland."

I returned to the kitchen and sat polishing in a stunned and stupefied silence.

"Where've you been? I was looking all over for you?"

I knew Mrs Murphy would challenge me. I couldn't tell her the truth and I hate to lie. Especially to her, on account of her dead sister and her kindnesses, but I had no choice. "I locked myself in one of the bedroom water-closets upstairs. Accidentally," I added when I saw the size of the

73

frown and the league of questions that were about to follow. "Sorry," and I dipped my head back into my work, giving it the elbow grease.

Mrs Murphy humphed and disappeared and I was left in peace to muse and dream.

How I wish Pat was here. How I wish I could tell him of all the secrets and mysterious events I have to write about in my diary, for I have no one to confide in about these happenings. Edward a Nationalist, and not a Loyalist as I would have thought. Have I really made such a wonderful friend?

April 5 1846

Two threatening effigies were found nailed to exterior doors up at Errill Manor this morning. I didn't clap eyes on them myself because they had been removed by the time I arrived, but one had been hanging from the scullery door and the other was out the back, in the yard, close by the stables. I didn't ask, for I feared to know, but I suspect one effigy might represent Edward's father and the other is a likeness of Edward himself.

Edward's father arrived at dawn this morning. I feel sure that those who pinned the menaces to the doors knew he was returning from London and intended to threaten their absentee landlord, not welcome him!

Gerard, the head gardener, and both stable boys, Hugh and poor pock-marked Dominic, were called in to be interviewed by the master himself. Everyone was on edge. I could feel the atmosphere. But can Lord Boulton really expect that, even if certain members of his staff did know a thing or two, they'd spill the beans to him? It would be an act of treachery. All over Ireland, landlords are throwing their tenants off their land. Do they expect that millions of poor Irish are going to turn a blind eye? Ireland will not go under without putting up a fight. Lord Boulton is the enemy now, even while he's the boss.

Even if Lord Boulton has leased his land to a middle man, I believe he still has a responsibility to us. He could show kindness. Surely he could waive his rents and insist that the middle fellows waive theirs too, until there is food again on our tables? He could open up his own grain stores. He could cancel all rent arrears.

But Lord Boulton has cold, ruthless grey eyes and I hold out no hope of generosity from that quarter, even if he is Edward's father. No, he has washed his hands of all responsibility but assured himself of a regular income. While we, his tenants – for, essentially, we are his tenants because we live on his land, whatever system they think up – we have been delivered into the greedy hands of others.

Edward's sweet good looks and civilized ways must be gifts from his mother. I wonder was she English as well? I pray that Edward is safe from whatever plots may be afoot. For if the worst should happen, who apart from me knows which side Edward has chosen to fight with?

April 6 1846

Da fears revolution – "The place is ripe for it," he says. Every night as I lay my head down, desirous to sleep deep, all over the land there are those, including my own lost brother, who are plotting deeds too dreadful to think about. Who knows, in the very dead of Tuesday night Pat might have been close at hand, stalking the yard at Errill Manor. Did he pin those effigies to the doors? Even if not, even if he is far away from here, wherever he is, he will be about resistance work. I pray to God he keeps himself out of harm's way.

I fear for the safety of those I love. For different reasons, they are all in danger. Ma is ailing, Mutt is dying, Pat is dicing with death and treason and Edward could be slaughtered in his bed for no crime other that he's the son of an English landowner.

April 7 1846

No work today. I am glad to stay at home, to help with the little 'uns. I hadn't noticed how neglected they are all looking. I worry for Ma's weakening chest. She coughs blood but, when I ask, she denies it. She's as thin as a cornstalk with dark rings round her soft beautiful eyes. Her face is lined. It's puzzled and sad. I could weep for her one minute and take up arms the next.

Da says I'm to get rid of Mutt. "Lead him down the lane and lose him on the roadside or take him to the river and drown him. I don't want that blasted animal breathing his last here. The young 'uns'll be fussed by it." But I cannot do it. I carried him up to the Ring of Elms, where I saw the beggar family a while back. He weighs no more than one of those fine linen sheets I've seen Mrs Murphy laying on the beds. I rested him on his side under the trees and he lifted his head an inch or two, breathing hard, and looked up at me with those great grey eyes and I knew I couldn't abandon him. I'd rather die myself.

"Oh, my Mutt," I says to him, caressing his soft floppy ears. "You wouldn't harm a hair of my head, no matter what, and I cannot hurt you neither. But what are we to do?" And then I decided upon a plan. Tomorrow morning, I shall carry him across the fields to Errill Manor and hide him in the stables. He'll be no trouble, and a bed of straw will keep him warm and comforted. He's too weak to run wild and make a fuss. With a bit of luck, everyone will think he belongs there. I'll see him every day and I can steal him scraps. Though, Lord knows, these days there is no such thing as a scrap of food. It's a meal to some living soul.

April 8 1846

Edward and I have barely uttered a word to one another since the arrival of his father. I feel as though our exchange in the library never took place, as if I dreamt it. I see the two of them together in the drawing-room in deep discussion and I wonder what they are talking about. Why has his father returned? Is it because of the troubles? Are they planning their escape?

Everything is splitting in two. We are taking sides, even those who don't choose to. It's inevitable. The country is starving, that's a fact. There are those who have food and those who have nothing. Those who have a roof over their head and those who are in the gutter.

Oh Lord, what if his father has turned up here to take Edward back to England with him? I couldn't bear it. *Edward.* He is in my thoughts even more than Pat these days. . .

Ma's coughing something terrible. I hear her hacking away in the night. She's not been right since Eileen passed away. She never mentions Pat, for fear of making Da angry, but, like me, she pines for him.

April 10 1846

Crossing the yard this morning at Errill Manor, fists clenched and squidgy with stolen grease scrapings, I heard my name called in an urgent whisper. "Phylly!" I turned guiltily and there was Edward in riding clothes striding towards me. My heart soared at the sight of him but I felt awkward on account of the food squashed and oozing in my fingers. The grease scraps were not mine to take. Officially it was stealing, which makes me a thief like Mary.

"Where are you off to?" he asked.

In my haste, I'd forgotten the slop pail which was to have been my excuse for crossing the yard.

"To the stables," I lied.

"I'll come with you. I want a word."

I turned my head this way and that to see who might be observing us. Any onlooker might ask what business Edward Boulton and I could have together. On top of that, I was not on my way to the stables but to the disused barn on the far side of the grass enclosure where I have Mutt hidden, warm in the darkness. I nodded, eyes averted, and took another step. Edward drew close. I had never encountered him out of doors before and now, to be walking at his side, was both exciting and confusing. My heart was thumping like a bass drum.

"Do you have chores in the stables these days, Phylly?"

"Not exactly." I did not want to lie to Edward but I was unsure how he would react to what I was up to.

We reached the stables and there was Hugh, in the shadows, running his blackened fingers over one of the dappled-grey mare's rear hoofs, looking for a nail or something. The mare whinnied. When Hugh glanced up and saw Edward and I together, he frowned, looking quizzically from one to the other of us. I moved on quickly, almost tripping over my bare feet on the cobbles.

Edward followed directly after me. "Where are you off to? I thought you said the stables. . .?"

"To the barn behind the chicken coops." I did not wait to explain and broke into a trot.

Edward caught up and kept step with me. "I need to talk to you, Phylly." He seemed troubled.

"Give me a minute, please."

When we reached the disused barn, I disappeared inside and was instantly swallowed up in the darkness. It felt safe. I breathed deeply. Mutt, recognizing my scent, began to whimper. I fell on my knees and shuffled towards where he lay. The straw beneath me rustled and his tail swished contentedly. He mewled with pleasure as he greedily gulped the bits of dripping in my hand. I lay at his side. I wanted to caress and reassure him for he spent hours in here alone and I feared that he would begin to believe that I had abandoned him, but I dared not linger.

"Whose dog is that?"

I had not heard Edward approach and had trusted that he would remain outside. I scrambled to my feet.

"Please, don't be angry, Edward. I know Ireland is starving but I couldn't leave him to die. What I give him would barely keep a bird alive."

Mutt's tail was thumping against the straw-covered earth at the prospect of more company.

"Where did he come from?"

"He's mine. Don't make me send him away, I beg you."

Edward smiled. "Your nature is generous, Phylly, and loving. Let the dog stay but you are right to keep quiet about him. There may be some who will not take kindly to his presence here." Then he took me by the arm. "Phylly, I must speak with you."

Aside from the day in the library when Edward had

shown me his Repeal Card, his fingers brushing against my hand, he had never touched me before now. I began to shiver and I knew it was not the sunless shed.

"My father has returned," he said.

As he led me through the darkness towards the daylight, I told him that I had seen his father on several occasions. On reaching the entrance, we both of us paused, hovering within the hidden safety of the interior, as though some instinct warned us both that our friendship was already out of bounds and might, any day now, be judged dangerous.

"I must leave." He seemed to be speaking to himself as though I had been forgotten.

"Leave?"

I could not bear the thought of it. Our friendship brought me so much happiness. Without him, my days would lose their purpose, and yet I knew this was utterly foolish. And wrong. I had my family to consider. They must be my purpose. One day, I couldn't picture when, but some day in the future when there was food again and independence in Ireland, I would stroll down by the river again with Pat, talking nineteen to the dozen and listening to his passionate romancing. But for now the struggles were only made tolerable by my dreaming and in all my dreams, Edward featured.

"Are you leaving for England with your father?" I asked, for he had not responded to my first question.

"Of course not, Phylly. Haven't I told you already that Ireland is my home. You must trust that. I have a duty here. But my father is insisting that I return with him. . ."

My heart sank. It was as I had feared. Whatever he said, Edward was going to be lost to me.

"And so, I must disappear for a while. Until father has given up on me and returned alone to London."

I said nothing, trying to face what he was telling me. I had lost Pat and now I was about to lose Edward. *Please, take me with you!* These were the words my heart cried out, but I did not voice them. I had my family to consider. We could not survive without the pennies I was earning and my mother, whose health was growing poor, needed my support for the chores. Pat had gone, following his heart-felt convictions, so it was my duty to stay.

"Thanks for not saying anything about the dog. I better get back or Mrs Murphy will be looking for me and Mutt will be discovered."

Tears stung my eyes as I hurried out into the bright daylight and sprinted across the tufted grass and the cobbled yard towards the refuge of the scullery and my work.

April 15 1846

Edward is still living up at the manor. Every morning, when I arrive, I fear hearing the news of his departure, but as each day passes my heart grows a little more quiet. Was it only idle talk? I cannot ask him for he has not tried to find me and I dare not go to him. Yesterday, Mrs Murphy made a comment about young girls flirting with their masters and how it was an improper way to carry on. I blushed and stared at the floor, certain she was referring to me. I've lost heart for writing and intend to put this diary aside. I shan't share secrets any more. What's the point? I feel low in spirits and Ma hasn't stopped coughing all evening.

April 24 1846

Da and young Hughie have got themselves signed up for one of the Board of Works projects which have been organized by the British government. The idea is to create work rather than give charity.

April 26 1846

Da was exhausted when he got back. It was well after dark. He says the overseer of the works bids them spend the days hauling heavy stones up and down a series of hills to a site where others are digging ditches. A road is to be built. Da says it doesn't seem to head in any particular direction. He's not bothered though. The cash earnt will help us buy victuals throughout the coming summer. "It's better than begging," he said, which is what we might have been reduced to without this help. We are all counting the days to July when the new crop will flower white and healthy. We giggle and fantasize about digging FAT potatoes out of the earth! Soon, this hunger will end.

April 30 1846

Gerard took me to one side this afternoon and told me, hushed-like, that Pat is well and living in Tipperary!

"Whereabouts?" I cried, astonished. The north of Tipperary is not so very far. I could walk there on my next free day. Oh, to spend sweet time with my brother again!

"I couldn't say where, but tell your family that he is safe," was all Gerard would confide. "You have a brother fighting for Ireland's freedom, Phylly. Be proud of that and don't you forget whose side you are on."

I suspect Gerard knows more than he is owning up to. It's so hard to know who stands with who. For who would ever have thought that Edward is on our side? But how stupid I am! I was so taken up with the news about Pat that I did not pay attention to the rest. Gerard was warning me. There must be gossip about Edward and me. I am being judged for spending time with an absentee landlord's son!

How it will cheer Ma to know that Pat is alive and close by. I long to give her the grand news, but not tonight. Tonight, I won't wake her, for she's sleeping soundly.

May 1 1846

"You are to be questioned. Come with me." That was Mrs Murphy's greeting when I arrived this morning. I supposed it was because I've been late three times this week, on account of Ma, but it had nothing to do with that. "A silver candlestick has gone missing!"

I trudged the corridors at her heels to Lord Boulton's study. As we entered the room, dark with wood panelling and heavy green curtains, His Lordship was looking out of the window. He turned and strode to his desk.

"You may go, Mrs Murphy."

Mrs Murphy bobbed a curtsey, gave me a withering look and disappeared, leaving the door ajar. So she could eavesdrop, no doubt, but Lord Boulton's no fool. He noticed at once.

"Close the door, girl," he ordered sharply.

I obeyed and returned to face him. My palms were sticky. I was hot from running across the fields and my heart thumping. I was *scared*. Even though I'd done nothing wrong I felt guilty, and feared it showed.

"What is your name?" His Lordship seated himself behind an enormous mahogany desk. His expression was stern. His fingers drummed the desktop in front of him. I was so nervous I couldn't remember my name and almost blurted out Mary! Not to lie, but because she was in my thoughts. I was thinking it must be she who had swiped the candlestick.

"Phyllis McCormack, Your Lordship," I stammered.

"Do you know that stealing is an offence punishable by transportation?"

I nearly fainted with shock. "But I haven't stolen anything!"

"Nothing at all?"

I remembered the fat drippings and pictured poor Mutt in the barn and how I had given him morsels scraped off dinner plates. Was that stealing? True criminal thieving? Could I be punished for that? They'd been talking in the kitchen about how dozens of youngsters were being transported for the filching of precious more than a loaf or a hemp rope.

"I am waiting, girl, for your answer? Have you stolen from this house or not?"

"No, sir."

"If you own up, I shall treat you with leniency. You will be dismissed in shame but you will not be prosecuted and transported. If you do not own up and I find you out to be a liar, then so be it. You will find yourself on Spike's Island prison, hands and feet chained, waiting for a ship to carry you to Van Diemen's Land where you will doubtless pass the rest of your miserable days, distanced from all family and loved ones." His voice with its clipped, English accent was dry and cold.

The picture he painted was enough to force anyone to own up to a crime they had not committed. My knees were knocking. I wanted Edward here to defend me. I longed for Pat. I feared Lord Boulton knew about the scraps for Mutt.

He fixed his steely grey eyes on me and I swear he took pleasure in my fear. "I haven't stolen, sir," I reiterated.

"Be off with you then," he said.

I scooted to the door.

"Wait! Are you the girl who has been idling away her time in the company of my son?"

I swallowed, agitating my fingers against the brass knob. "I've spoken to him once or twice, sir." Who had reported such a thing?

"You are paid to work, girl. Now get out of here before I dismiss you for your lazy Irish nature."

I bobbed a curtsey and fled, closing the door hard behind me. I was relieved to be out of there but my blood was boiling with rage. No person deserved to be spoken to the way Lord Boulton had just spoken to me.

Back in the kitchen, all eyes settled on me, including Mary's lovely gaze. She was carrying a basket of dirty linen and must have been on her way to the laundry room.

"Well?" Mrs Murphy spoke, but it was to Mary I turned. I knew she was entreating me not to give her away.

"I haven't taken no candlestick," I said, and strode off to fetch my pails.

Later, just as I was finishing off my broth, Mary found me. I was out in the yard, perched on a stone pillar, with my broom at my feet. I'd chosen to sup my soup alone because there were confusions inside me that I needed to straighten out quietly. In any case, it was a warm sunny noontime and I preferred the sunshine to the cool shade of the scullery, and solitude to the gaggle of staff. The heat put me in melancholy mind of the summer past. Before the potato blight, when Pat was still at home and I'd passed carefree days bathing in the warm reedy river with him, secure in the glorious belief that life would always be wonderful, that no evil would ever come to harm us.

I didn't think that way any more and at that moment I doubted that I would ever know such happiness again.

The interview with Edward's father had left me with a horrid feeling. I was heavy-hearted for so many different reasons, but now I was also insulted. Me and my family are poor and hungry but there's no shame in that, and being Irish is something I am mightily proud of. Yet His Lordship had spoken to me as though all those factors added up to a nobody. I was remembering Pat and his rage against the British and their treatment of our island and although I had always sympathized with his opinions I had never actually *felt* that angry about it. Now, I did.

"There you are. I've been looking for you."

Mary's soft voice made me jump for I hadn't been aware of her approach. Too deep in thought I'd been, with my head tilted skywards, staring up at the birds flying free, asking myself what such liberty felt like. A heart so light that I might float above the clouds!

There was no other pillar for her to sit on so she crouched on the cobbles at my feet.

"You were quizzed about the candlestick then?"

"I was, and I'm suspected."

"You judge me for it?"

I shrugged, for I certainly did, but the blueness of her eyes beseeched me to think the best of her. And for my part, what did I care how much she stole from Edward's father?

"Don't let him catch you. He'll show you not a scrap of mercy. He's threatened me with transportation for it."

"Well, he doesn't have to fret about the feeding of a small child who's always hungry, not knowing nor understanding potato blight. You'll not give me away, will you, Phylly?"

I shook my head. "Stealing's a sin though, Mary, remember that. Whatever the circumstances."

"They stole our land in the first place! We'd not be in this sorry state if the land belonged to us and we was not paying crippling rents. You must know that, Phylly."

"Sure I do."

"That brother of yours must have told you. He's with us. He's fighting for Ireland so you better not let him down."

I turned my gaze upon her and was puzzled by the strength of her passion but, uppermost in my thoughts, was how and what she knew of Pat for I had never mentioned him to her. It reminded me of what Gerard had said about Pat being safe in Tipperary. Was it only me and my family who had heard nothing of him?

"What do you know of my brother?" I asked.

Mary dropped her eyes and scratched at the cobbles.

"Have you news, Mary? If you have, I'm begging you to share it."

I waited until, eventually, she whispered, "He's wanted, Phylly."

My heart began to beat furiously. "Wanted? What do you mean *wanted*?"

"Mrs Murphy said as not to say anything to you on account of your ma being sick and you anxious."

This information stunned me. I pictured all the staff gathered around the big wooden table in the kitchen, hungrily devouring their bowls of soup and gossiping nineteen to the dozen as was their wont. But about *me*! Such a possibility had never dawned on me. Where had I been while those conversations had taken place?

"Well, you've said something now so you can't leave it at that. In what sense *wanted*, Mary? Speak up or don't count on me to keep your secrets for you." I spoke without thinking for I had no mind to threaten her. It was the need to hear news of Pat. "Sorry, that didn't come out right."

"The military are after him. He's in hiding."

"In Tipperary?"

She nodded.

I felt tears sting my eyes. "I'm so glad he's alive," was all I could say at first and then, "What's he wanted for?"

"Ribboning. They'll come down heavy on him if they catch him, but he's a brother to make you proud, Phylly."

May 2 1846

I crept in to Ma this morning before setting off for work. She's pale and feverish.

"Pat's in Tipperary," I whispered, feeling the heat and clamminess on her cheek as I brushed my lips against her ear. "He's safe and well."

She tilted her beautiful face towards me, her eyes brimming with expectation, and I felt a burning lump in my throat. I was reminded of Mutt when he was all but dying beneath the elm trees before I carried him off to the barn.

Is Ma *dying*? Never, until now, had I considered such a terrifying possibility.

"Ah, Phylly," she rasped. "I'd give the world to see him walk through that door. . ." and then she began to cough something awful, blood dribbling from her lips. I dabbed at it as best I could with the skirt of my stained and tattered shift.

"Hush, Ma." I wiped and soothed her hot, sticky brow with the palm of my hand. Her long brown curls were damp and bedraggled, her flesh parchment-pale.

She closed her eyes as though my touch had brought her peace and I prayed the news of Pat had eased, not troubled her.

My walk to work through the fields was heavy of foot. I stopped more than once to gaze round about me. How is it possible that a land like ours, so rich in natural beauty, can produce such a depth of hunger and sickness? But I found no answer to my philosophizing. For sure, both Pat and Edward would have answered me with a thousand reasons, all of them political, but at that moment I could not see the world through their eyes. All I could see was cruelty and life's injustices and I trudged on weeping for my mother's pain, and for myself.

I have not so much as glimpsed Edward for days, but no one has mentioned anything so I cannot think he has gone away. Where can he be? Every day when I sneak out to the barn to feed Mutt, I hope he'll be there waiting for me, but he never is. It is only my stupid fantasy.

May 10 1846

My birthday. My diary is one year old today. Am I really only fifteen? I feel that this last year has changed me greatly.

May 14 1846

Mary has been arrested! The constabulary came for her today, four uniformed men, knocking at the kitchen door. "You are under arrest," cried one, and grabbed her roughly. Poor Mary began to weep hot tears for her little Lucy. The kitchen was silenced. No one stepped forward to help. Not even me and for that I am ashamed, but I could not think how to defend her. I know that she is guilty. Guilty in the sense that she stole, but NOT GUILTY because she needed food for her hungry child. Edward has to persuade his father to drop the charges and give her back her job. But where *is* Edward? Who will look after Mary's baby? Does she have family? Life has grown so cruel.

May 15 1846

Edward was in the library this morning! I had to stop myself from running to greet him. I long to speak to him; there is so much I have to say but nothing feels safe any more. I must wait for him to approach me. It is a month since we last talked together.

May 17 1846

The gossip at the lunch table today was of Mary. She has been taken to a prison in Tipperary town. Her case will be heard at the quarter sessions where she will, almost certainly, be found guilty and deported. It seems that the magistrates and juries come down more heavily on those who steal from their masters and employers. So, her chances of being kept in prison in Ireland are very slim.

If I knew where Pat was hiding, I'd set off to find him and visit her as well. She must be feeling sick in her heart at the prospect of what lies ahead. A transportation ship to the other side of the world! No one up at the manor seems to know if her daughter is with her. I did not dare enquire about the child's father and I wonder now why I never asked Mary about him. I hadn't wanted to busybody in her private life, I suppose, and I'd had plenty enough cares of my own.

Hungry as I was, I could not swallow a mouthful of my soup as I listened to the description of her being chained to a cart with a dozen or so others who had committed like crimes and driven away.

I set my bowl back in its place and wandered out from the kitchen. I had nothing for Mutt but I went to visit the barn anyway. I needed the comfort of his company and hoped he would forgive me for arriving empty-handed.

Alone, in the darkness, I lay alongside him, stroking him and whispering to him and tears fell down my face. Imagine if I had been blamed for Mary's crimes and taken away on that cart to Tipperary prison. I feel so sad for her and her future.

"Am I hearing tears, Phylly?"

I could not believe it. It was Edward's voice coming softly at me through the shadows. I lay still, not answering. I couldn't speak. "Phylly? It is you, is it not?" He was drawing closer. Mutt struggled to his feet to greet him but I remained nuzzled in the dog's fur, hiding my tear-stained face. I heard the rustle of the straw as Edward knelt down. He rested his hand on my head and stroked my hair. We remained like this a few moments and I felt soothed by his touch.

"Where have you been?" I asked eventually.

"Dublin. You should have been there, Phylly. There were times when I wished you were."

So, he had not forgotten me entirely? Oh, I felt SO happy to see him again. I have lost count how many times I have wished him here with me. I turned shyly towards him.

My eyes were stinging and puffy. A stalk of straw had stuck to my wet cheek – I must have looked a sight – but Edward slid his hand from my hair and brushed it away.

"Hello, Phylly," he whispered. Mutt leant across me, licking Edward's fingers. The dog dribbled down my face but I didn't care.

"I've missed you," I blurted out, before I'd thought to check myself.

"I missed you too. You would be inspired by all that I have heard and seen, Phylly. I've witnessed Thomas Meagher's oratory firsthand. I stood before him, surrounded by Young Irelanders, and it's a thing I'll never forget. Now, I know in my heart what my head has long since told me. Ireland is where I belong and what I must fight for."

Disappointment washed over me. Had Edward missed me only because I am his friend, his country-girl comrade? Do I represent the people, his cause? Or has he missed me because he loves me as I love him? None of these questions were answered. They were not even posed, except in my thoughts.

"So what of England and your father?" I asked. It was safe ground.

"If he will not listen, will not allow me to lead my own life, I shall tell him that I agree to go to London."

I sat up fast. Mutt mewled and resettled a few feet away from me. "You'll go?"

"Sssh, Phylly, when will you have patience! No, I will

make him believe that I have agreed. Then, I will set off alone either before or after him – I will find some pretext or other for not travelling with him – and then I shall make directly for Dublin, take rooms there and begin my work."

"What work?"

"I have allied myself with the Young Irelanders. I will either write for the *Nation* newspaper or they will find other employment for me. The nature of the work is not important. As long as I am with them."

"But what of your studies, Edward?"

"There's time for that when Ireland is free and she is her own mistress again."

I should have been joyous for Ireland, for Edward's passion and commitment but – and I can write this here because this diary is for the most secret of thoughts and for no one's eyes but mine – my concerns were personal, jealous ones. I want Edward to be *for* Ireland, but I don't want to be loving someone as obsessed as Pat. Of course, I had never looked at it like this before but imagine loving Pat, not as a sister, but as a girl who is attracted to him. There is no place in Pat's heart for girls. Ireland is his love and it looked to me as though I had chosen someone with that same commitment. I rejoiced for Ireland but felt disappointment for myself.

I must learn to be patient. I'll be Edward's russet-haired, freckled companion, if that is how he sees me, anything to stay close to him, and pray that, when Ireland is liberated and her people are fed and living in dignity, he will discover that he loves me. It's the best I can hope for now. I shall be Edward's loyal friend and I'll wait for love.

May 20 1846

Since Da and Hughie have been roadbuilding they do not get home till all hours and Ma is left with only the little 'uns to care for her. This has been worrying me but I saw today that Grace, who has turned nine now, is a great strength. She's funny and cheers Ma with her mischievous, jokey ways. I don't think my sister knows how comical she is as she tells stories, chatters and mimics folk. Father Timothy popped in this evening to bring Ma Holy Communion. He muttered something to me about Pat but I pretended I hadn't heard and he didn't repeat it. I wonder the Church is not doing more for the people. Couldn't they organize themselves and stand up against the British government?

May 25 1846

Da looked worried this evening. He confided that he and Hughie have not been paid since their second week of work. I could not believe it! Rather than starve or receive charity many people have signed up for the works programmes – so many that the supervisors cannot keep track of them all. Surveyors are employed to measure the daily workload performed by each labourer but they are not able to keep abreast of it all. On top of which, there is insufficient money to pay the wages. It makes my blood boil. Da is humping heavy stones and wearing himself to the bone and we have nothing to show for it. His breathing is all wheezy too. Fortunately, Hughie is not troubled by the labour.

June 3 1846

As I was walking home this evening across the fields, I spotted Edward crouched against the trunk of one of the big oak trees, reading. He said he had been waiting for me and offered to accompany me. Although I knew that I should not dally, on account of Ma, we sauntered, taking pleasure in the warm, sunny evening. The fresh young growth on the trees shone golden-green in the sun. My heart felt light, until Edward told me his news. A place at Cambridge University in England is being kept open for him, to study law.

My step faltered. I took a deep breath. "Your father must be pleased," I rejoined, trying to get a grip on my emotions.

"Yes, he was delighted when I showed him the letter."

"When must you leave?"

"If I were intending to go, which I am not, I would begin my studies in October."

We walked on a few steps in silence; dry summer grass crunching underfoot.

"I am leaving for Dublin tomorrow morning, Phylly."

"*Tomorrow morning!*"

"You sound surprised, but I have told you of my plans."

"Yes, you did. So now . . . now your father knows of your desire to work in Dublin and not return to London?"

"No, he would prevent me. As it is, he is insisting that I return from Dublin in a month, to prepare my departure to England. Of course, I shall not return."

"No, of course not." My heart was sinking. When would I ever see him again? "Are you to be employed by the *Nation* newspaper then?"

"Only humble tasks, Phylly, in return for a floor to sleep on. I shall deliver and fetch and assist John Mitchel, the editor. I will be there where the Young Ireland movement was born and I shall learn the ways of newspapers and journalism. It will be a grand adventure."

"It will, and I wish you all the best," I said, struggling with the lump tightening in my throat.

His news delivered, we came to a stop in the middle of the track, tall grass brushing against our feet and ankles. Edward laid his hands on my shoulders and looked hard into my face. I felt the sun on my freckles and pain in my heart.

"Take grand care of yourself, Phylly. I will write and you must promise to reply."

We embraced like brother and sister and said our goodbyes. I could not help but notice the excitement, the cheerfulness in Edward's eyes. I wished him well, agreed to stay in touch and went on my way. Edward's prospects, whether in England or Dublin, are rosy. Our worlds are a million miles apart.

June 13 1846

Twice the sum the British government has allotted as an alms grant to Ireland has been given over for an amusement park in a suburb of England, visited by Londoners, called Battersea.

Edward has been gone nine days. I have no will to write in my diary. I miss him terribly.

June 17 1846

No news from Edward. I stood in his library today and recalled past moments there. Even with all those books, it seemed an empty space.

June 20 1846

At last! A letter from Edward, in his own hand, addressed to me, care of Mrs Murphy. She handed it to me in the kitchen when we were alone. I caught the look in her eyes but it was not as judgemental as I might have dreaded. Can she know who it is from? I have never in my life received a letter before! I could barely stop my eager and trembling fingers from ripping it open but I tucked it away in my shift as though it were a thing of small importance, hiding my impatience and quietly relishing the news to come.

Early this afternoon, concealed behind the barn where Mutt is hidden, I sat cross-legged on the ground. My four-legged companion dozed at my side as I leaned against the exterior wooden wall, gazed out across acre upon acre of Boulton land and then opened *my* letter. Here is what it says:

My dear Phylly,

How many sheets of paper would it take to describe to you all my news? What exquisitely full and exciting days I am living! I have been attending the weekly Repeal meetings which are held in Conciliation Hall. The Young Irelanders, including my hero Thomas Meagher, are heartily resisting the proposed alliance between O'Connell and the Whigs. Meagher made a rip-roaring speech which all but matched O'Connell in oratory. Meagher is a handsome and dashing figure of only 22. Yet how he took command of that room! Would that I, four years hence when I am the same age, have the courage and spirit that I witness in Thomas Francis Meagher and his comrades. It is an honour to work for these men and to fight alongside them. You should be here. . .

I glanced up as a cream butterfly fluttered past and I stroked Mutt's greying fur. How I wish I might walk the streets of

Dublin city with Edward at my side. What a dream that would be!

There are many who claim that our undisputed Irish leader is still Daniel O'Connell but there are almost as many who see Meagher as the brave voice expressing the growing concerns of the majority. As you know, Phylly, my vote lies with Meagher. And then there is William Smith O'Brien who is no longer standing between O'Connell and Young Ireland. He is wholeheartedly with Young Ireland now. My chores are, as I had expected them to be, of a fairly humble nature but I do not care a jot. The offices of the Nation are crammed with articles and legal books and writings, and young men passing to and fro arguing amiably. There are one or two rather extraordinary young women who occasionally drop by. They are contributors of articles, mainly poetry. I see that my life has been far too sheltered for I have never encountered such splendidly elegant, outspoken creatures! They have each chosen a nom de plume (a professional writing name) which seems to add to their charm.

I stopped reading at this point for a moment and thrust the letter angrily into my lap. Oh, Edward! Am I to lose you, not to England or the cause, but to an elegant young lady who writes verse?

We are receiving reports here in Dublin that the famine has taken such hold that Peel's Indian corn depots are being opened against strict instructions from London and that the meal is being sold to starving families who are being obliged to sell off whatever clothing they are wearing to purchase it. Such a shocking fact, don't you agree?

We, Young Irelanders, are here fighting for the political and human rights of our nation but it is so important for us to remember that the vast majority no longer care a jot for politics. Their minds and ravaged bodies are taken up with one desperate thought: food, and how to get hold of it.

I hope that you and your family are surviving these tough days. I feel quiet in the knowledge that you have a salary, such as it is, and that your father and brother are also employed, though it seems there are thousands working on the Board of Works projects who have not been paid. One report claimed that several have died while at labour because they were without money to buy food. Such a scandal.

Write to me, Phylly. I long to hear news of you and all those close to you.

Your dear friend,

Edward

I folded up the parchment page and slipped it inside my shift. I was contemplating the blue sky and the clouds passing before me on the distant horizon while my mind echoed his final line: *Your dear friend, Edward.* What had I expected? A love letter?

June 24 1846

Eleven weeks till we begin harvesting the new potato crop. Then this famine horror will be at an end, but Edward spoke true: I and my family have employment. We are a great deal more fortunate than most.

June 30 1846

My dear Edward,
I do not have the excuse of such full and rewarding days as you for the length of time this reply has taken me. Still, my chores have been demanding and in the evenings I am tired.

Did you hear that your father has returned to London? I do not know if he is intending to come back to Ireland in the near future or to await you there. No one has mentioned it and I cannot ask, for your secret is of course my secret and I have not uttered a word about your whereabouts to a soul. With neither you nor your father in residence, Mrs Murphy is ruling the roost and seems mightily content!

My mother is very poorly. Fortunately, the few shillings I have earnt over these past six months has meant that we are not entirely destitute and, as I am given my bowl of vegetable soup and bread at midday, I can go without at home, although eating so little weakens me and leaves me tired. Da and Hughie have still not been paid for their work; weeks now they have been digging ditches in this summer heat. It seems that the reports you are hearing about men dropping dead while labouring because they have no money to feed themselves are entirely true. I have been trying to persuade Da to give up the work but he remains convinced that at some point in the near future he and Hughie will receive the wages due to them. I am not so optimistic, for the surveyor has resigned saying that he can no longer keep track of who is owed what, nor what has been achieved or by whom. Does Westminster know of this mess? Why not write an article about it for the paper? I have little other news except that I dream of seeing the streets of Dublin city. I pray for your well-being. Write soon.

Your Phylly

July 14 1846

"Find Pat, Phylly, and tell him to come to his ma one more time." Oh, how my heart buzzed at my mother's words. Buzzed like an insect enraged and trapped in a container that it cannot get free of. I could not bear the thought of what she was suggesting and tried to convince myself that it was her fever babbling, but I am no fool. Her eyes looked watery and far away.

I left Ma with Grace and went directly to Mrs Murphy who said that she was sorry to hear my mother was ailing so bad.

"Will I lose my position," I asked her, "if I go away for a few days and fetch Pat?"

"Have you a clue as to his whereabouts, child?"

"I was thinking to try Tipperary."

"Tipperary's a big place, girl. How do you intend to find him?"

I shrugged. I was going on Gerard's remark about Pat being spotted there, but that was weeks back and I did not want to mention Gerard to Mrs Murphy in case this information linked him to a secret society.

"Who's going with you?"

"My brother, Hughie," I lied.

Mrs Murphy watched me chewing my bitten nails. I could tell she was considering my situation.

"There's no master here to know of your absence," she said, "so there's no reason not to pay you the few miserable pence they give you when it's due. I feel sure it's what young Master Edward would instruct, were he here. . ."

I tried not to catch her eye for I feared she would expect me to return this kindness by sharing a titbit of gossip, but I could not give Edward away – not at any cost.

"Thanks, Mrs Murphy," I mumbled and made to go. And then I remembered Mutt. In the old days I would have taken him with me for protection and company. Now, I knew he hadn't the strength for such a journey. In any case, where was I to find food for him? But if I left him alone in the barn, having no notion how many days I'd be gone, he might die of starvation and Da would kill me if I took him home. . .

"Phylly, have a word with Gerard."

I turned in surprise. "What about?"

"You'll find him in the walled garden. If it's locked, shout to him. And before you set off, come back here."

Entrance to the red-brick garden was by a wooden door. A key had been left in the lock so I stepped inside without need of calling and paused. The air was heavy with a close heat and the smell of ripening fruits and vegetables. My stomach and senses had grown used to so little and to such plain food, that the luscious scents made my head dizzy. A distant thud led me to Gerard who was digging at the far end of the garden. As I approached, a swarm of flies beyond him busied themselves around a hillock of manure and the humming of bees collecting pollen buzzed in my ears. They were not going hungry!

"Phylly!"

"I have to find Pat," I said briskly, for the warmth and the unfamiliar aromas made me want to swoon. "Do you know where he is?"

"Tipperary," Gerard said, dropping his fork to the ground and wiping the perspiration off his wrinkled, sunburnt brow.

"Do you know where?"

"Go to Mullinahone. You'll find him there."

"Where in Mull—?"

"It's a small place. You'll find him."

I thanked him and made my way back along the narrow paths that encased the vegetable beds. I was wondering how much more Gerard knew.

"Good luck!" he called. I waved and disappeared. So many all across Ireland are dying from starvation and sickness, including my own mother, that the sight of so much produce on the estate troubled me.

Back in the kitchen, Mrs Murphy had made up a cloth parcel for me. She was hurrying to and fro, flustered, as though it were she embarking on this journey. "There's food for you both for a few days. Guard it close or you'll be robbed for it. I'll have victuals sent over. Your family won't go without. You won't be eating your daily ration so I'll pass it on. Soup for your ma, there'll be. But you come back soon or I'll have some grand explaining to do, do you hear me? It'll be my livelihood at risk."

I nodded, as I gathered up the rag of food she had prepared. Her barking words quite hid the kindnesses she was showing to me and my family. I hurried to the door. I had one more chore to arrange.

"And Phyllis. . ."

"Yes, Mrs Murphy?"

"We'll feed that blasted dog for you. Now, get on your way."

After hugging Mutt hard and reassuring him that he'd be fed proper and that I'd be back before he missed me, I scooted across the fields, burying my food bundle in my skirt. It was getting towards 11 o'clock. I intended to be on the road before midday.

When I arrived, Grace was at Ma's side relating a story and Ma, eyes closed, was smiling – but not too much because laughing makes her cough.

"Where's Mikey?" I asked Grace.

"Down by the river hoping for a fish."

"Tell him I said to behave. I'll see you in a day or two."

Alarmed, Grace jumped to her feet. "Where are you going?"

"Sssh, you'll disturb Ma. Here." I handed her Mrs Murphy's food parcel. She looked puzzled. "It's from the big house." I had taken out one chunk of bread and pocketed it. I preferred my family to eat the rest. I didn't want to be robbed and none of us profit from it. "Ma," I said, crossing to her sleeping place. "I'll be back with Pat. Keep your strength up, please."

She nodded without opening her eyes, and I kissed her.

While I was searching for this diary and my pencil, Grace came after me. "Does Da know what you're about?" she whispered urgently.

I shook my head. "Tell him not to fret. I'll be back with Pat the first moment I can," and then I embraced her and hurried off into the warm, late-morning sun determined to think only of what lay ahead and not of those I was leaving behind.

July 15 1846

Crossing into the barony of Tipperary took me until the evening yesterday. I passed by the outskirts of a small town

114

called Templetouhy and sat for a while by the river. The landscape is lusher here, rich agricultural land. Looking out over the hills, it seemed so peaceful I could almost have persuaded myself that this is not a country torn by famine.

Last night I ate half of my bread and I slept on hay in the outhouse of a stone barn into which I had crept for shelter, but I barely closed my eyes because it smelt horrid and I was a bit afraid. I found some unripened blackberries this morning, green and hard, but they provided me with breakfast. Today, I walked fast, heading south, stopping barely at all, except to drink water from a couple of streams along the way. I passed through several villages with many abandoned homes. Starvation is written across the faces of those sitting motionless by the winding roadsides. Quite shocking. I met many beggars and, once or twice, I was tempted to give up my bit of bread, but common sense stayed my hand. For if I do not eat I won't have the strength to reach Mullinahone. The bread has grown stale now, which is better because it takes more chewing and my stomach thinks it's receiving extra. It is quite incredible that I am doing this all alone.

July 16 1846

Scores of people are scouring the countryside looking for food and I myself am feeling weak this evening. My stomach is screaming but I have no bread left. I didn't cover as much ground today. I had counted on arriving in Mullinahone this evening but was slowed by a range of hills to cross, Slieverdagh.

Tonight I am sleeping in the open. Thank the Lord, the weather is dry and I am not obliged to lay my head on damp ground. It is chillier here in the hills because of the altitude but the stars are bright. I am looking up at the heavens now and dreaming of Edward in Dublin beneath this selfsame sky. My mental pictures of him give me confidence.

I am longing to clap eyes on my own dear brother again. Still, I set off on this journey rashly. Desperate for Ma and fearing for her sickness, I was thinking only of reaching Pat. I dare not guess what Da's words were when he returned and found me gone. It comforts me to know that Mrs Murphy will send over rations.

July 17 1846

I reached Mullinahone early this morning but no one had heard of Pat. Eventually, I knocked at the church. A parish priest can be counted upon to know the comings and goings of all his parishioners, but when I asked after Pat, this plump fellow screwed up his eyes, looked at me fiercely and began to interrogate me. "Why are you travelling alone? Have you lost your family?"

Fingers crossed behind my back, I nodded, hoping he'd have pity and feed me, which he did in his big kitchen. God forgive me for the fib! I scoffed the bread and cabbage soup greedily but studiously avoided his and his housekeeper's questions, except to admit that I had trekked 40 miles from Queen's County, south of Roscrea.

"It's vital I find my brother. He's staying in Mullinahone. Surely, you've seen him?" I did not add that Pat's probably in hiding, yet I had the distinct impression that the mention of his name ruffled the fat priest. For the twentieth time today I described Pat's blond hair, his tall muscular frame and dancing eyes, but the priest only glared mistrustfully. His housekeeper, behind him, did not meet my gaze. Their behaviour made me suspicious.

Later, I sat on the ground outside the church listening to the bells tolling, wondering what to do next. Why would Gerard have sent me all this way if he hadn't been certain Pat was here? I should have found out more information when he gave me that first clue weeks ago. Stupid, to have set off so unprepared. I was feeling anxious about Ma and wondered if I should begin the hike back home. On the other hand I didn't want to go back without Pat, or without news of him at least. It would break her heart if I did.

If his base was somewhere in the vicinity, how was I to find it? It was a tricky business. Might Pat have been arrested? After I left the church, I trawled the central streets of Mullinahone again and chanced upon the police station. Screwing up my courage I enquired within, but had no better luck there. The disappointment decided me. I'd hasten north and make for home after quenching my thirst at a pump I'd spotted in the market square. It was there that I caught sight of the priest's housekeeper hurrying along the street. Without seeing me, she turned down a lane and disappeared into the noon heat. I called, but she didn't hear. So I chased after her, reaching her as she slowed outside a small white cottage. I must have startled her because she rounded on me and snapped, "Why are you following me?"

I was taken aback by her lack of kindness. It is not the usual Irish manner. We pride ourselves on our friendliness towards strangers. Even in these difficult times, I would not have expected a person to speak so harshly. It confirmed my suspicion that she and the priest knew more than they were letting on.

"My ma is ailing bad. She's begged me find my brother and bring him home to see her once more."

Her eyes, boring into me, showed no compassion.

"If he's in trouble," I gambled. "I'd better know it, for I must return with news."

"The constabulary have him and the others with him. He'll be rotting in the gaol by now, no doubt about it."

Mary's breathless words as she crouched on the ground at my feet all those weeks before, the day Lord Boulton interrogated me, began to haunt me. "*He's wanted, Phylly.*"

"Which gaol?" I asked weakly. I was thinking of the uniformed men who'd knocked on our door and spoke of transportation for crimes against the English.

"Tipperary, I shouldn't wonder."

I turned on my heels without a thank you. It was gone midday when I made my way out of the small town, asking directions as I ran. "Which is the road to Tipperary?"

"Keep heading west. It's a straight road once you reach Cashel."

I gave Pat's name to several. They shook their heads or averted their gaze. I have the feeling their sympathies do not lie with Ribbonists.

"Is it far?"

"A day's steady walking."

So here I am, making for the gaol at Tipperary. If Pat's there, it'd be better to know it. If not, I shall visit Mary. One extra day on the road will not lose me my job, nor cause Ma and Da to fret any the greater.

July 18 1846

It has taken me less than the full day to reach Tipperary. Along the highways and byways, I have passed dozens of families of squatters huddled outside their sod huts or scouring the fields for any sort of food. Poor souls. Many are living in ditches dug by the roadsides with nothing but a few clumps of turf and bits of broken branches to protect them against the seasons. High on a windy hill, I passed a cart carrying a dozen or more naked bodies. Victims of famine and typhus, to be sure. Children and adults. It brought to my mind little Eileen, whose passing seems a lifetime ago yet in reality was only a few months back. Thank the Lord, it is only a matter of weeks to the new harvest.

Tipperary gaol is the first I have ever stepped foot inside and it turned my stomach. I explained that I had come in search of my brother, gave Pat's name and waited while the doorkeeper thumbed through pages of names. Eventually, he shook his head. Desperate as I am to find my brother, I was greatly relieved because it gave me hope that Pat may still be at liberty. Then I enquired after Mary. The wizened keeper ran his finger down another list. Eventually, he nodded. "She's here."

"May I visit her?"

I was led along corridors by a woman keeper with a limp and a hacking cough. There were no exterior windows and the place did not smell too good. Each corridor was fair to bursting with visitors – relatives and families, I think. I was surprised to see so many children inhabiting the cells with their mothers. Women were pressed up against the bars, wailing, while their small children screamed and slapped tin plates against those bars.

"What are they doing?" I called to the crippled woman who was guiding me.

"Demanding food," she answered, without a glance towards the prisoners or me.

As we wended our way down corridor after narrow corridor, moving towards the very heart of the place, the echo bouncing off the stone walls grew more fierce and exaggerated. Particularly the incessant clanking and turning of keys. I caught sight of Mary before she noticed me and I held back before calling because I was so shocked by her appearance. She was pale and as thin as Ma, and the blue brightness of her eyes had dimmed markedly. Her face was tense with fear but when she spotted me she looked greatly cheered. The great iron key was turned and she stepped out of her cell. We embraced like long-lost sisters.

"What brings you to Tipperary, Phylly?" Picking out Mary's softly spoken question was not easy amidst choruses of screaming voices echoing in every direction.

"Searching for Pat. My ma's gravely ill."

This news seemed to depress her for she suddenly dropped crouching to the ground, buried her face in her hands and her whole body began to shake. It took me a minute to realize that she was crying. I bent and stroked her hair.

"I don't think he's here."

"Thank the Lord. What's your sentence?" I asked gingerly.

"Transportation. Fifteen years."

My stomach lurched. "Fif. . . Why so long?"

"Because I was found out for the candlestick, which was silver, and because Lord Boulton made no plea for mercy on my behalf."

I closed my eyes in shame for I had not spoken to Edward, not lifted a finger to help her.

"The blessing is that Lucy will come with me."

"How much longer must you stay here?"

"Until I'm allocated to a ship. Then I'll be taken to whatever port the boat is harboured at and imprisoned in that place until the ship is ready to take prisoners on board. I may have to live weeks in the hold waiting for the ship to sail, only walking the main deck once a day. I fear the lack of fresh air and natural light. Some get sick or die during the voyage, for it takes several months. And the rats! I'm scared of rats! Oh, Phylly, I pray to God they don't have a ship available and they leave me here. I dread being transported. Don't stare, Phylly, please. . ."

"Sorry, I. . ."

"I know you warned me stealing is a sin and I wish with all my heart that I had heeded you, but it's too late now. I stole to feed Lucy."

While she spoke I was asking myself what justice could condemn a mother and child to such a sentence? We said our farewells. I hugged her tight and heard her sniffling in my ear.

"You've no news of Pat then?"

She shook her head.

"Is he operating out of Mullinahone?"

"No, he and his five compatriots disbanded and went off in separate directions after the parish priest gave up their names to the constabulary. They're wanted for treason."

"The priest!"

"Yes, he and others of the Church fear that if the English are angered by Irish anti-state activity, they will suffer. The British government helps the Church fund their training colleges."

"How do you know all this?"

"My husband, Thomas, is one of the five wanted with Pat."

Now I understood why she had been left with no one to fend for her and the baby and why she had been reduced to stealing.

"I'm grateful you came," she whispered. "I'll always remember you for the kindness." And with that she turned and was instantly swallowed up within a moving mass of women. I did not wait but pushed my way forward out of that monstrous place.

July 20 1846

Most of those women prisoners are first-time offenders. Most have been convicted for stealing. In almost every case, their crimes were committed to make money to buy food for their families. The system pays no heed to their reasons. To my poor way of thinking, it is very harsh.

It's no matter that I'm a *colleen*, I feel anger heating up my blood. If I was a *gorsoon* I'd fight for Ireland! *Gorsoon* is an Irish word for boy. Thank the Lord, I'm on the road home.

July 20 1846 – evening

The scene before my eyes must be the most pitiable misery
I shall ever be obliged to witness. I have returned home this
evening to find our cottage *burnt to the ground* and *my family
gone*. There is barely a stick of evidence left – no more than a
few smoking cinders – to say that we ever lived here.

July 21 1846

Yesterday, after the shock, I beat a desperate path to Errill Manor,
to learn of my family. It was dark by the time I arrived. Mrs
Murphy took me in her arms and held me tight before leading
me into the kitchen and sitting me in her big wooden chair.

"Where are they? Are they safe?" I begged.

She shook her head solemnly. "We've no news, child."

Although I was worn out from walking, and starving
hungry, I could not be persuaded to eat. I was trembling.

"When did you see them last?"

"I sent Dominic over with soup at midday," she said. "Soon he was back, blathering about the place burning fast and not a soul in sight. They must've fled."

Mrs Murphy crossed to the scullery door and yelled to Dominic to come in from the stables. I was trying to take it in, to picture the scene. How would my mother have walked? Had Da and Hughie been there or had they returned later to find the house burnt and the family gone? That was unlikely because it was past sunset when I got there – the hour Da returns from work. I'd have seen him, surely.

Dominic appeared, followed by Gerard. They looked grave.

"What do you know?" I pleaded.

"There are two other homes burnt up near the Ring of Elms," Dominic replied softly.

"It's landlords' doing," added Gerard.

"But we weren't in arrears with our rent!" I wept.

Mrs Murphy heated me a broth while the others sat with me. I was in shock. I drank it and then rose. "I best be going," I said.

"Where to?" she exclaimed.

"I don't know, but I've got to find them."

"Stay here tonight. In the morning, we'll sort something out."

Exhausted, I accepted her offer.

First thing this morning, accompanied by Dominic because Mrs Murphy refused to let me go alone, I returned to the ashes of our home and stood for a while staring at those charred remains. A horrible thought occurred to me: what if my family had not got away in time? But it was clear that this was not the case and I thanked God for it.

Half of Ireland is homeless, starving and sick – I have seen it with my own eyes during these last days – and every blessing must be appreciated, but I was feeling mighty sorry for myself. What was to become of me? There was Pat on the run, Mary in prison, Ma sick and my entire family disappeared without trace. How would I ever contact them again? The situation felt overwhelming. I bent my head and wept.

July 22 1846

Today I walked to the Ring of Elms and found the other burnt homes. No traces of habitation or life left anywhere. From there I hiked to my parents' friend and neighbour, William. To think that only one year ago we were all dancing and singing in our yard while he played the fiddle. His wife, Mary, is pregnant with her first, God help them.

"They were driven out by the rent collector. Your da sent Hughie to us to leave news for you and Pat," William explained.

"It seems he'd been keeping money back secretly, fearing

for your ma's health and the rising price of food. Apparently, he'd visited the rent collector and begged for lenience and time, but had been warned that he would be shown no favours."

According to William, our shortfall was not considerable, unlike the other families who had paid nothing for a year. Still the same charge of "rent arrears" was made against us and so our humble farm was taken from us and burnt.

"A party, including the rent collector, came on horseback soon after dawn. Your family were told to take any belongings they wished to save, vacate within the hour and be clear of the Boulton estate by noon, never to return. Any neighbour found harbouring any member of an evicted family would be shown the same treatment."

"But where are they now?"

"Walking to the coast."

"How will Ma ever make it?" I cried.

"They won't be alone. Thousands of dispossessed families are doing the same, hoping to scratch an existence out of seaweed and an occasional fish. Many are dreaming of buying a passage to America or Canada. It seems that the American people have heard of the terrible times we are living through and societies are being formed to create support. Irish families are being welcomed into these new lands."

"Did they say which coast?"

"No, but it'd be Dublin no doubt. Hoping for passage on one of the emigration ships."

I sat silent in our neighbours' snug cottage and tried to picture my family on the road somewhere. And if they found a ship, to which country would they go? I thought of all my own dreamings of America. A great landmass, wide and filled with opportunity. How many times had I recounted this dream to Ma? If they were fortunate enough to find the means to leave, surely they would pick America. But how would I ever, in all this world, find them again?

I thanked William and Mary, retraced my steps to the big house and passed on the news to Mrs Murphy and Gerard. Then, I recounted all that had passed during my visit to Mullinahone and Tipperary gaol. Gerard said that if Pat and his comrades had been arrested, it was likely they would be imprisoned at Kilmainham Gaol on the Liffey river, bordering the city of Dublin.

Mrs Murphy offered me shelter again in her room, which is where I have slept these last two nights, but I told her that tomorrow I will leave from here and, grateful as I am to her for so many kindnesses, tonight I prefer to sleep out with Mutt. I can wrap my arms about him and weep without disturbing anybody. In any case, she has shown me such generosity that I would hate to endanger her position should Lord Boulton return unexpectedly and find me living under his roof.

Now it is night and I am curled up in the barn with Mutt. Tomorrow, I shall set off for Dublin in search of my family but, if all else fails, I shall go to Edward, for who else is there left for me to turn to? Mrs Murphy has promised that she will listen out for news of my parents. (Everyone here at Errill Manor has been so generous.) I have given her the address of the *Nation* on the understanding that not a word is breathed to Edward's father. (It's strange. I search everywhere for my kin and Edward is running from his!) Mutt will stay here. He has a home on this estate and the walk to Dublin will be a hard one. One day, when life shows a kinder face to us all, I shall return for him. Alas, I cannot picture that day now.

July 23 1846

Dearest Edward,

So much has happened to change my life since last I wrote that I really cannot think where to begin. The long and short of it is that I am leaving Errill Manor this very morning for Dublin. It is possible that my family are in the city somewhere and I must try to find them. When I arrive – I have no idea how long the journey will take me – will you welcome me as your friend and help me find a place to stay until I am reunited with them?
Your very own,
Phylly

Mrs Murphy has promised to make sure my letter gets taken with the mail.

July 24 1846

I talked to a family on the road today who are also walking to Dublin. They are intent on buying themselves a passage to New York in America. Their name is Kennedy and they, like my own family, are farmers. We spent the night at Abbeyleix.

The Whig Party have gained power under the leadership of Lord John Russell.

July 26 1846

Ma's birthday. I cannot allow myself to dwell on it.

The Kennedys were also evicted and warned never to return to their homestead. One of the sons – Liam is his name – told me that the cost of the passage is around £3.5s for each ticket and half price for little 'uns. For those wishing to emigrate to Canada, it is cheaper: a little over £2. We are approaching Port Laoise. The going would be quicker if we were all less hungry and in better health.

July 27 1846

It is very strange how *un*alone I feel on this walk. People from many parts of Ireland are converging, seeking a means of escape. Unlike my trip to Mullinahone, where I was an outsider observing the effects of the famine, here I am a part of the mass movement. It is a true exodus. I listen to the stories of strangers and learn what has driven them out of their homes. I feel bonded with them because it is almost always the same tale. "The tyranny of the landlords", they are calling it and that is exactly what it is. The worst offenders seem to be the absentee fellows. Lord Boulting and his like. It seems that many of them have never set foot in Ireland! I wonder, will the British ever look back on these days and hold their heads in shame?

July 28 1846

In the fields along the roadside, all around Port Laoise, *the potato plants are blossoming once more!* The white flowers swaying in the breeze are like carpets of snow. What a glorious and pacifying sight! Before too long, there will be food again and there will be singing and jigging and fiddling in every hamlet across the land. For those who have not already lost their homes, have not fled the country or died of starvation or disease, the bitter times will shortly be over. Scars will be slow to heal, but there will be hope and a spirit of rebuilding. Ma, once fed, will get well again and I will be reunited with my family.

I have made two new friends, both about my age. Peter MacGuire and Thomas Dillon. There are many youngsters on the roads: famine orphans like myself. Sharing the walk stops me dwelling on all that has happened and keeps my loneliness at bay. Both have their sights set on America's eastern coast – New York or Baltimore. "But if the ticket is cheaper to Canada, why not go there?" I asked. Thomas explained that many in Canada speak French not English, but most importantly, it is ruled by the British whereas America is a free nation. I had not considered such matters.

At the sight of the acres of healthy crops, there are a certain number who are turning back, gambling that they will be allowed to rebuild their homes. I intend to continue north to the capital, although my feet are beginning to bleed from so much walking.

July 29 1846

I have been talking to another fellow-traveller, Michael O'Grady. He is the youngest son of a poor farming family. They are packing him off to make his fortune in America so that he can send money back to buy them all tickets out. He tells me the Chancellor of the Exchequer has ordered all public works operations to be shut down by August 8. "But will the people be paid for the work they have already accomplished?" I asked. He was doubtful. It brought Da and Hughie to mind and my eyes pricked with tears. How I worry for the welfare of my family. I cannot look much longer upon the sights that pass before me. I feel as though I have lived seven lives in the course of one summer. Pat was right. This little book, my diary, which I had thought to consecrate to my love for Edward, must tell another tale.

July 31 1846

Passed through Kildare this morning. I must wait back a day to rest my feet. They are very cracked and caked in dust and blood. Peter and Thomas offered to keep pace with me but I refused. We are all hungry. I don't want the responsibility of others' lives – or deaths – on my conscience. But I was sorry to say goodbye to them.

August 2 1846

Reached Naas. Dragging myself along. It is only the hope of finding my family and setting eyes on Edward again that gives me the strength to keep moving.

August 4 1846

No! No! NO! The potatoes everywhere are black and withered. Fields of blackness. Dead and rotten, putrefying before my eyes as I travel from place to place. In the space of less than a week, hope has turned to despair. I am seeing farmers digging in a frenzy with their bare hands to lift potatoes from the earth before they rot. Surely now, Ireland will starve in its entirety. Who or what can save her poor damned people? What nature of God could blight an entire nation of God-fearing folk for a second year running in such a cruel and unthinking way?

I have been separated from those I love for too long.

August 5 1846

Dublin city! I have arrived. My first ever sighting of the sea! It's a curious thing to be at the edge of a land looking out towards a watery horizon. It changes my perspective altogether. The idea of leaving this troubled island, of stepping off and crossing the waters, seems much more real from this bustling port. It is as if I could fly like the birds.

Suddenly I am reminded of the time I was in the courtyard at Errill Manor at noon, gazing heavenwards and watching the swallows, when Mary came looking for me. Poor Mary, I wonder where she is now. Is she still waiting in prison or aboard a ship bound for the other side of the world? Thank the Lord that, whatever horrors I have lived through so far, I still have my liberty. Please God, the same is true for all my family, including Pat.

Now, I am standing on the cobbled stones on Custom House Quay. It is a remarkable sight and the grey-stoned custom house itself is a magnificent building. Agents are buzzing about everywhere, selling tickets for the boats to Canada and America. If I'd had £2 and more in my pocket I might have been tempted, but I wasn't sorry not to have the money because I could not leave yet.

The queues for the ships tail back towards the city and must be more than half a mile long. I have been weaving my way urgently in and out of the long procession of expectant people, but there is no sight of my family. Could they have left these shores already? Are they at sea somewhere, bound for that distant unknown land? From here to America is 3,000 miles across the ocean.

The gossip amongst the congregating masses is of

widespread demonstrations and rioting throughout many of the Irish baronies. Mobs of starving labourers are marching on towns demanding to be employed. In one area, the labourers were so angry because their works programme had been cancelled that they tore up the stretch of road they had just laid.

August 6 1846

I am reunited with Edward! Yesterday evening, after I had trawled the streets for hours on end, peering into faces crouched in doorways or lying on the ground, everywhere enquiring fruitlessly after my family, I eventually gave up for the evening and walked to D'Olier Street, to the rented offices of the *Nation* newspaper, and the only address I had for Edward. My heart was pounding as I arrived at a crooked building with a rather undistinguished entrance and climbed narrow wooden stairs to a first-floor landing which smelt of newspapers and print. Beyond the closed door, I could hear the hum of lively chatter. I knocked. What if Edward had moved on? I would be destitute. Moments later, I was being greeted by a handsome but tired-looking fellow with shirt-sleeves rolled above his elbows. "Can I help?" he asked with a broad grin.

I gave Edward's name and was about to explain that I

was a friend from Queen's County when a shout rang out. "Phylly!" And Edward all but leapfrogged across the crowded room to greet me. He picked me up, swung me in his arms and deposited me inside the office. "I have been waiting for you!" Within minutes I was being introduced to the boss, Gavan Duffy, the one who'd opened the door, and a friendly bunch, most of whom are barely older than Edward. The space was cramped and chaotic: stacks of papers in every corner, desks littered with notes and scribblings and, beyond all of this, stood the all-important printing press. "The heart of our revolution, Phylly," whispered Edward when he saw me try to take in my surroundings, my eyes big as saucers.

August 7 1846

This morning Edward presented me to John Mitchel, the lawyer son of a Presbyterian minister from Ulster. He has blazing eyes and could charm birds out of trees! "He's the most remarkable and gifted of the *Nation* journalists. His language is intense and his desire for revolution merciless," said Edward.

They were discussing the split with O'Connell. A week or so ago, at a Repeal meeting, William Smith O'Brien – followed by Meagher, Mitchel and Duffy – stood up and walked out.

August 8 1846

A miracle has happened! A real once-in-a-lifetime MIRACLE! Edward led me to Burgh Quay this evening, to Conciliation Hall, headquarters of the Repeal movement and a short walk from the D'Olier Street office. The place was packed. O'Connell was due to speak, followed by Edward's hero, Thomas Meagher. Edward is right; he is spectacularly dashing!

I am not so tall, and the excited crowd was crushed tight against me. It forced me to stand on tiptoe so as not to miss what was happening. Daniel O'Connell rose to speak. There was a respectful hush. His strong voice silenced the smoky room. He spoke of Repeal but he insisted that the only way forward was through peaceful means. At this point, certain members of the crowd grew impatient and began heckling him: "Your policies are outdated!" they were shouting. O'Connell, who is over seventy now, grew agitated and answered back to the crowd. The crowd began shifting.

I was turning this way and that, witnessing the scene and greedy to remember it, when to my utter joyous amazement I heard a voice from the back of the hall: "You are losing the support of your own people, O'Connell. Our way forward is with Young Ireland!" I would probably have keeled over, but the place was so packed there was nowhere to fall. I thrilled to his voice before my eyes lighted on his person. There he was, standing high above the crowd at the front of the gallery, arms raised above his head like a fiery crusader.

"Pat! Pat!" I yelled. Tears streamed down my hot cheeks. My voice was drowned out by a hundred others shouting for Ireland and for our future, so I shoved and forced my way to where he was standing. I lifted my arms, waving crazily, but Pat did not notice me. And then the roar of the people all around me grew deafening as Thomas Meagher rose to his feet, but the politics were lost to me now. My eyes and mind were on one thing only. The living breathing sight of my dear brother, standing head and shoulders above all others.

"Pat!" I screamed, and then passed out from the heat and emotion.

The faint was a great bonus because it parted the crowds. Edward came hurrying to retrieve me – until then he hadn't even noticed I'd disappeared – and Pat's attention was drawn to the kerfuffle taking place beneath him. As I opened my eyes my blond-haired brother was leaping from the gallery and landing, on his knees, at my side.

August 9 1846

Pat and I have spent the whole glorious day together, chattering and exchanging news. It is a miracle that he is not in prison. He's wanted for treason which terrifies me, but he assures me that he is safe in the city. He had not heard of the troubles which have beset our family.

"I pray they're on a boat to the New World, Phylly," he said. "This is no place for them now, but we who are left must fight for Ireland's freedom."

"Ireland is starving, Pat. People have no strength left to care about freedom or politics," was my reply. We sat by the waterside on one of the quays, dangling our feet, and it reminded me of our sunny days fishing for salmon by the river. Pat's revolution is no longer in his dreams. It is in his blood and chills me to observe it. Though I have written of my resolve to fight for Ireland, when I look at my brother, I realize that such a thirst for fighting is not in me. I am tired and miss my family. Still, I thank God I am reunited with the two young men I love best in the world. Edward joined us this evening. He and Pat talked ceaselessly. Their vision and passion unites them.

No one could wish for two finer companions. Edward says that I can work at the *Nation* and that will feed me.

"What about Pat?" I asked, but Pat shook his head.

"My destiny is not with a newspaper, Phylly."

He must have seen the look on my face because he laughed and promised that we would not lose one another again. "I shall stay close at hand." Then he disappeared into the dark Dublin night, leaving Edward and I to make our way back to our lodgings.

I am sharing a room with four other young women. One, like me, is helping out at the *Nation*. As we said goodnight on the landing, Edward took me in his arms and hugged me. "It's so good to have you here, Phylly," he whispered, not wishing to wake anyone. His words thrilled me but his embrace left me wanting, for it did not express the same longing that I feel for him. He has missed me but not as I have missed him and it breaks my heart to know it. I wept as I curled up in my corner to sleep. My tears were such a confused mix because, on the one hand, I am so happy and, on the other, I ache.

August 10 1846

I have been allocated a fine job. I am to read all the English newspapers and all the Irish ones too, and save the articles that are of interest to our own journal. Or any story that I think might be worth relating.

August 17 1846

The public works programmes are to be reopened, but the food depots are to remain closed. There are reports of heavy rioting in several districts. Around the ports, gangs are boarding ships to steal the food loaded for export. It does not surprise me. People will resort to whatever means they must to prevent themselves and their families from dying. The government says that responsibility should lie with the landlords. But some are bankrupt and, of the others, how many are willing to help us? Of course, certain landowning families, such as William Smith O'Brien's, are buying crops to feed their tenants, while others are cancelling all outstanding rents or giving time to pay, but they are the *exceptions*.

Edward sent a letter to Mrs Murphy and instructed her – no matter what his father might bid to the contrary – to use all vegetables and produce on the estate for the feeding of the staff and tenants. To his father in London he wrote: *I beg you to take pity and cancel all rents owed to you and insist that your tenant, the middleman in all of this, does the same. Charge not a penny more until the people have found a means of survival.* Would that the landlord who burnt our cottage and evicted my family had expressed such generosity.

August 30 1846

Drinking dens are being opened on many of the worksites of the Board of Works projects and now drunkenness is being blamed for the mob riots and uncontrollable labourers. I believe that liquor is not the root of the problem but despair, frustration and appalling work conditions.

September 4 1846

Edward and I work from dawn to night and I have so little time left to write in my diary. No news from Pat. I wonder where he has disappeared to.

September 24 1846

It seems that frequently, when the Board of Works labourers are paid, it is with one note between several because there are insufficient coins to pay each employee separately. This leaves them the choice of going to the drinking-shop to change the money or walking to the nearest town. Walking to town involves the loss of a day's work as well as the hardship of the walk itself, for which many are no longer fit, so the choice becomes the drinking den. Inevitably, sorrows are drowned, drinks are drunk and the one who gains the larger part of the wages is the publican rather than the poor devil who has dug from morning till evening for a few pence.

October 10 1846

Lord, it is cold – and not yet winter. I walk to work taking the route alongside the Liffey. Most mornings, I meet hordes of starving people. They are flooding into the cities from coastal areas and from the countryside, begging for food and hoping for work. Outside Dublin, they are dying by the thousands.

October 22 1846

John Mitchel told us today that bodies are lying like rags across the country. Deaths go unrecorded and, I dread to think it, even unnoticed. The poorhouses are fair to bursting with the droves arriving at their doors, screaming for food. Not a day goes by without I stare into blank unknown faces, thinking of my family.

November 3 1846

I cut this out of the *Cork Examiner* printed in yesterday's issue:

> *Talk of the power of England, her navy, her gold, her resources – oh yes, and her enlightened statesmen – while the broad fact is manifested that she cannot keep the children of her bosom from perishing by hunger. Perhaps indeed Irishmen may not aspire to the high dignity of belonging to the great family of the Empire; they may be regarded as Aliens. But when the Queen at her coronation swore to protect and defend her subjects, it is not recollected that in the words of the solemn covenant there was any exception made with regard to Ireland. How happens it then, while there is a shilling in the Treasury, or even a jewel in the Crown, that patient subjects are allowed to perish with hunger?*

November 15 1846

There are close on 300,000 people working on the public works projects now and insufficient staff to deal with such numbers. Starving women, with small children at their sides, are reduced to heavy digging work. I hear they are paid four pence a day for their labours, precisely the sum I earnt at Errill Manor though my tasks were far less strenuous.

Snow is falling in Tyrone. In all my years I have never heard of that. Millions are sick, starving, living out of doors and now they have adverse weather conditions to contend with. I am beginning to believe those who say this island has been cursed!

November 17 1846

The numbers dying on the public works are increasing. Even small children labouring for a penny are dying from cold, soaked to the skin and starving. Many have dysentery. What misery this is, yet still Charles Trevelyan, who is in charge of the Treasury in London, will not give permission for the food depots containing the Indian corn to be opened. He writes that it is better to wait until there is "real danger" of starvation! Has the man lost all reason? Or is this a more efficient way of killing off Ireland, an economical method of waging war? Edward warns me that I am in danger of growing bitter but it is not bitterness I feel. It is outrage. And frustration. Thanks to a priest in Tipperary (not the treacherous fellow I met in Mullinahone), drinking dens on public work sites are being outlawed. It seems that many of the publicans were Board of Works committee members!

November 20 1846

Here at the *Nation*, we are publishing lists of landlords who are reducing or forgoing their rents. Edward and I have been working into the early mornings compiling the lists. He looks pale and thin but works relentlessly. Sometimes, when I gaze at him, I wonder if it's the shame he feels about his father's uncaring attitude that drives him. We have grown so close since my arrival in Dublin. I am no longer the scullerymaid and he the landowner's son. We are comrades working towards the same goals – but how my heart cries out for more!

December 2 1846

Mobs of people – 5,000 in total – have attacked the workhouse in Listowel, County Kerry, shouting, "Bread or blood." For sure, the result will be blood. We hear that Charles Trevelyan has not opened the depots because there is *no corn* in them, and fresh supplies will not be here until the spring. God help Ireland.

A gorgeous dark-haired lady – perhaps one of those elegant beauties Edward wrote about in his first letter to me – visited the *Nation* this evening. I was tucked away in a corner, cross-legged on the floor, snipping articles out of yesterday's London *Times* when I looked up and saw her. Gavan Duffy rose from his desk to greet her. They kissed like old friends. Then she handed him several rolled parchments. Poems, I suppose. Gavan did not introduce me but, since I was buried beneath stacks of newsprint, it is possible he had forgotten I was in the room.

"Will you stay for a while?" he asked.

She grinned flirtatiously but shook her head, saying she had an engagement. Gavan nodded, rested a lazy arm across her shoulder and escorted her to the door. As she was leaving she said,

"Give my regards to that handsome Edward Boulton. I'm sorry to have missed *him*." I nearly cut my finger!

December 14 1846

Icy gales are blowing in from Russia, so cold that even the River Thames in London has frozen over. Out of desperation, farmers are eating the oat and corn seeds they had stored for planting in the spring. If the seeds are all consumed now, what will be left to grow and what effect will no crop have on Ireland's ability to supply its own food? Of course, the bitter truth is that during these past two years, while an entire nation has dragged itself around on its knees, crops have been produced in plenty and sold abroad for prices that no Irishman could have afforded. I am learning about market economy from Edward. His articles are being published regularly in the *Nation*, which is thrilling. His passion and commitment are inspiring, but dangerous. John Mitchel and Tom Meagher are his mentors. Both are encouraging him to continue with his legal studies.

I miss my family achingly. Where is Pat?

December 25 1846

We are spending the holiday at the office for there is always work to be done. It is perishing cold but we are fortunate because we have a fire burning in the black iron grate. I am usually the first to arrive so I have made the lighting of it one of my chores. The others, whose minds are filled with mightier problems, are grateful for it.

Through the window this afternoon, I have been staring at the snow. It is falling thick, flakes as big as autumn leaves. Droves of homeless wretches trek through it, hunched against the swirling wind, battling onwards to nowhere. Others are slumped in doorways, sleeping under bridges, huddled together like bundles of smelly sacks. Thousands and thousands are dying from typhus fever. No one is bothering to count anymore. What does Christmas mean to any of them? Dogs roam the streets in search of bodies to feed off. There are 400,000 people listed as being employed on public works now.

I have been weeping, wondering what has become of Ma. What of Da and my sister and brothers? What a year it has been. Dear Mrs Murphy is still feeding Mutt.

Pat dropped by to wish us well but his attention was diverted by that dark-haired poetess who arrived soon after him. Her name is Bridget. For her part, she seemed so taken with Pat's charm that she did not glance once in the direction of "that handsome Edward Boulton". Good old Pat!

I am trying to persuade Edward to find a horse and take me to Errill Manor for a few days. I long to tread the soil that was my home. Edward tells me that I must face the future and put my energy into that. Yes, but I need to believe that one day we'll all go home again.

January 2 1847

Edward received a letter today from his father in London.

...I am warning you that you are risking your safety, your liberty and your future career if you do not give up these political writings. Westminster is not going to sit back and allow such troublemaking Irishmen as Meagher, Mitchel and Smith O'Brien to poison the colony with

their rebellious preachings and plots. The British are not
blind to their influence and they will, ere long, seek ways
to imprison them for treason, and you, Edward, risk being
sentenced along with them. You will bring disgrace on
the Boulton name, if you do not extract yourself at once
from such an unlawful crowd. Finally, if you do not make
your way to England and take up the place being held for
you at Cambridge University, I shall cut you off without
a penny.

My skin turned to goosepimples when Edward read me those lines but his response was calm. "Phylly, it is the Boulton name that concerns my father. He cares not a jot for me or Ireland. Well, then, let him go to the devil!"

When everyone had left the *Nation* offices this evening, Edward wrote a brief reply to his father saying that he cares not a fiddle for his threats of disinheritance! "I have some money of my own, Phylly, and when that is spent, why then we must work like every other living soul." I love it when he talks of "*we*".

Just as we were leaving Pat arrived. We walked together, me in between them, by the Liffey river. Pat told me how pretty I have grown. "Aren't I right, Edward? Hasn't my young sister blossomed into a beauty?" I told him to stop teasing but Edward rested his arm across my shoulder and whispered, "Yes, you're startling to behold." How I blushed!

Later, when Pat had gone on his way and we had returned to our lodgings, we stood on the landing in the darkness. Edward took me in his arms and held me tight. Pressed tight against one another, I longed to whisper how much I love him but I contented myself with leaning my head against his chest, listening to his beating heart, and then he spoke words in my ear that I shall never forget.

"You know, Phylly, when our task has been achieved and Ireland is at last free, I want to return to my studies. I shall have no rights to Errill Manor, unless my miserable father has a brainstorm, and there is no longer a home waiting for you in Queen's County. Although I still have some funds, we have cut our cords. We are rootless souls, you and I, so we will need to build new dreams. Think what you want, Phylly, for there will be a future for us beyond the revolution."

I don't dare dream what he might have meant, but I cannot help my soaring heart.

January 4 1847

Trevelyan has finally given the order for the Indian corn depots to be opened, but is insisting that the corn be *sold at market price PLUS five per cent*! Even his most loyal staff are warning him that this is inhuman. Ireland cannot pay for the food, not at any price. His reply is:

If the Irish find out there are any circumstances in which they can get free government grants we shall have a system of mendicancy such as the world never knew.

I looked up the word *mendicancy*. It means: begging, or relying upon alms for sustenance.

Here's what I would like to write to Trevelyan:

Ireland is starving due to two successive years of potato blight, caused by circumstances beyond our control, and you, Mr Trevelyan, fear that gestures of charity to the sick and dying will make beggars of us! We are victims of a system which has grown out of the confiscating of our lands over the past several hundred years. It allows Irish land to be rented, then divided up, rented again, and then sub-divided into even smaller portions and rented again, each time at a more inflated price. The middlemen are the winners while those who toil the soil can barely make ends meet. They have no land to grow anything but potatoes and when hard times strike they have no rights against eviction. And in the light of this, Mr Trevelyan, you issue the order to sell the corn

in the depots at five per cent above the market price for
fear anything less will make us beggars! Where is your
heart?

It is more than twenty months since I wrote my first words on these blank unknowing pages. I was an innocent fourteen-year-old. I am still not quite sixteen. I have lost almost my entire family through sickness or eviction. I am living in a city I had never visited before, sharingmy days with friends whose every breath is breathed for Ireland's freedom and I realize that something fundamental has changed in me.

Prayers alone will not end this terrible time. When I return to Queen's County, I will not find everything as it was before. The lives of millions, including my family, have been scarred or destroyed. I can choose to face facts or I can continue wishing it were otherwise. But not even if I tear these pages into tiny shreds can I turn back the clock. Nor can I close my eyes or my heart to what lies before me. I am standing in front of my own destiny and my journey is just beginning.

Epilogue
September 19 1848

Anyone who picks up this already salt-stained book with its curling covers and begins to read might ask themselves: What happened? Regular entries for almost two years and then a gap of more than eighteen months with not a word written. Why?

Let me begin with the present and work backwards. I am safely aboard the *Harmony* and bound for Boston on the eastern coast of America. My very last image of Ireland was yesterday afternoon when I stood crushed on the crowded upper deck, with tears tumbling down my wind-chapped cheeks, waving farewell to the quays at Waterford and to my brother Pat, who was not there to wave back because we left him hiding in the hills of Tipperary five weeks back.

During a few short weeks this summer, in a last desperate attempt to force the British to give Ireland back to the Irish, Young Ireland and those who supported the cause gathered together and concentrated activities within the triangle of land that unites the counties of Tipperary, Kilkenny and Waterford in the south.

The British got edgy and sent in troops and warships. Many of the peasant people were willing to defend our cause, but few had arms. Some had pikes, handfuls were carrying muskets, others stones or pitchforks, but against a regular army what chance did we have? The weather was wet, our hopes were buzzing but none of us were warmongers and the British were determined to put a stop to us.

Even so, the days that followed were exciting, extraordinary and unforgettable – even if they finally got us nowhere.

We slept under the stars in the mountains of Slievenamon. One of my strongest memories of that late July week will always be the flaring beacons which lit up the night skies. One night Thomas Meagher burned a beacon to signal his whereabouts and within no time, all across the hills, others began to shimmer and flame. It was thrilling.

Edward and I never left each other's side. The love I have dreamed he would one day feel for me blossomed on those summer hills. I tasted my first exquisite kiss beneath the rush of a golden Tipparary moon. Sometimes we met up with Pat but he preferred to keep moving. Pat had been on the run a long time. The revolution was do or die to him. Everything was at stake. My brother is a brave young man. I used to think he was a dreamer skilled in romantic ideals, but I have come to know him better. His passion for his country's freedom is the heart that beats within him.

But our revolution has been a dismal failure. Thomas

Meagher was arrested and is in prison along with William Smith O'Brien. Both await trial, charged with high treason. John Mitchel has already been transported – he was found guilty of treason-felony earlier this year. His ship, bound for Bermuda, has probably already reached its destination. Gavan Duffy, arrested on several occasions, has so far managed to avoid conviction. As long as he is at liberty, he intends to print the *Nation* newspaper.

Saying goodbye to Pat was the hardest thing I have ever had to do.

"You take care of her, Edward, or I'll call you brother no more," he whispered softly as we left Tipperary on a fine warm morning.

"Count on me," was Edward's brief reply but I knew his heart was breaking like mine at leaving Pat.

Pat embraced me hard and then Edward and I went on our way without looking back. I could not for the tears I was shedding.

We made for the coastal town and busy port of Waterford. It took us the best part of six days, walking fast and resting only when we were too tired to go further. As soon as we reached the coast we went directly to the quays in search of a ship to America. Within a week we found passage, in steerage, on this splendid three-mast sailing vessel, the *Harmony*.

Food was impossible to come by in the town, even with a little money to buy it. I learnt from a bedraggled, scrawny stranger who asked me for a farthing, that rations were given out daily at a nearby soup kitchen. It was there in the queue that I caught sight of my little sister, Grace. At first, I thought my breaking heart was deceiving me for she has changed immeasurably. She is no child now. She is thirteen – almost the age I was when I started this scruffy journal.

"Grace!" I yelled.

Clutching one another tight, shivering with shock and disbelief, we wept at the sight and feel of one another. Then she led us back down cobbled lanes to the dockside where I looked upon my father for the first time in two and a half years. Hughie and Mikey were at his feet, huddled like dogs against a seafront wall. They have been taking turns to visit the soup kitchen, bringing back anything they could beg or scratch for Da who is too weak to move and looks like a skeleton.

Darling Ma died on the road, less than a month after our cottage had been razed. Da, heartbroken, would not leave the spot for months. They lived in that ditch until the winter set in. Then, slowly, with her spirited humour and courage, Grace herded them south with the promise of a ship, but they had no funds for passage and, of course, could find no employment. In Waterford they remained, living on the rocks by the docks.

Edward has paid all our passages even though his money

162

is dwindling fast. When Da thanked him for it and for taking care of me, happiness choked my throat. Edward's reply was: "I hope always for the opportunity to care for Phylly, sir."

When we arrive safely in our new land, I shall paste my ticket in this book. Here is what is writ on it:

We engage that the party herein named Phyllis McCormack will be provided with a steerage passage with not less than 10 cubic feet for luggage, for the sum of £4, including head money, if any, at the place of landing, and every other charge. Water and provisions according to the annexed scale will be supplied by the ship as required by law, and also fires and suitable hearths for cooking. Bedding and utensils for eating and drinking must be provided by the passenger.

The water ration is six pints for each of us every day – that's for washing, drinking and cooking. We are fortunate to be leaving before the harsh winter weather sets in. For, as we sail towards a new world and a new life, the cholera has struck the potatoes again; the fourth year in succession. Ireland has grown weak and disorganized. The population has been cut by *three-quarters* as a result of death, transportation or emigration, and our Emerald Isle has become a sorry, desperate place.

September 20 1848

This morning the sky was clear and the sun was shining golden as I strolled the deck with Grace and Edward. Even with the sea breezes the temperature is mild.

"How long will we be on this ocean?" Grace asked me.

"Eight weeks."

"Oh, Phylly, that means Christmas in America!" she whooped.

"I pray so," says I, gazing at the sea. It gives me such a sense of release.

Suddenly, we saw grey slippery creatures frolicking and diving near the boat. "Look! Look! What are they?"

When Edward told us they were seals, Gracey clapped and jumped. Her happiness is a joy to behold. She laughed when she saw me watching her and asked me in whispers whether Edward and I intend to marry when we reach America. "He loves you so," she said. "It shines out of him. And look what he has done for us all."

"It's rude to whisper and you know it, young lady." I chided, but smiling.

"If you don't tell me, I'll ask him."

"Perhaps one day," I laughed, and hugged her tight, for I still cannot believe the miracle of being reunited with my family. My sorrow is Pat. If only he were with us, but he has chosen to stay behind and fight on and I must respect that, though God knows what will become of him.

Aside from him, I still think of Ma and Eileen and Young Ireland, and the many whose names have not appeared in my little account of this terrible episode of history – brave men and women who have died, been transported or are awaiting trial. All of them had a dream of a united free Ireland and all of them have in one way or another given their lives to it. God bless them. I pray for peace.

Historical note

In 1841 a census showed that the population of Ireland was over eight million. About half of these Irish people worked on the land, farming potatoes for food. Some were able to farm small quantities of other crops which they sold. Potatoes were popular because one acre of crop could just about feed a family for a whole year, with enough "seed potatoes" left over for planting in the following year. Most small farmers and their families lived on their potatoes, with very little other food in their diet. The money gained from selling other crops, or an animal, was used to pay rent to the landowner. The potatoes were harvested in September/October and the crop could be kept for about ten months. June, July and August, when the potatoes from the last year's harvest had run out, were known as "meal months", the hungry months, when people would have to find money from somewhere to pay for other food.

In 1845, a fungal disease, which became known as Potato Blight, attacked the Irish potato crop and destroyed about a third of it. In the following year, nearly all the potatoes planted were killed by the blight. In 1847 the effects of the disease were less severe, but many people had been forced to eat their seed potatoes, so the crops were very sparse, and in 1848 the disease destroyed almost the entire country's crop again. The blight was less harsh in the next two years, and by 1851, when the worst of the disaster was over, the Irish people were attempting to rebuild their shattered lives.

The peasant people who relied almost entirely on potatoes suffered the worst hardships. During the years of famine caused by the failure of the potato crop, one million people died and another 1.5 million emigrated to other countries to escape the hunger. A smaller majority of the population were transported to Australia or Van Diemen's Land (later to become known as Tasmania) for crimes such as stealing or riotous behaviour.

Many of the deaths were due to starvation, but the vast majority of people died from diseases like typhus, dysentery and cholera. Whole families were wiped out, and many more were split up as a result of the famine, which was at its worst in the west and southwest of Ireland.

Much of the farming land in Ireland was owned by landlords who lived in England and rarely visited their estates. Many of the landlords, though far from starving themselves, were facing financial ruin as a result of the famine because few people could afford to pay the rent due on their land. Some of the landlords found a solution to this by simply evicting the tenants from their homes and letting the land to people who could afford to pay. The evicted families were left to fend for themselves with no shelter or means of support. Over 13,000 families were evicted in 1849 and 14,500 in 1850.

The British government introduced some measures to help the Irish people during the famine. In 1846, Prime Minister Robert Peel imported corn from America to be sold from government depots in Ireland. In some parts of the country the corn was the only source of food, and people attacked the food stores because they were so desperate to eat. Public works were set up, employing men to build roads that were not always necessary, so that they could earn money for themselves and their families. But wages were poor, men already made weak by hunger often had to walk great distances to get to work, and pay was sometimes severely delayed, if it arrived at all.

The Soup-kitchen Act of 1847 set up soup-kitchens all over Ireland to feed people directly. Over three million people a year received badly needed food in this way. Private charities in Ireland and England also did their best to aid the starving Irish people. Although all these measures helped to some extent, they were too little and too late to stop the worst effects of the famine.

The potato famine focused attention on the repeal of the Act of Union. Passed in 1800 – against the wishes of the majority of the Irish population – this British government act united Ireland with England and Scotland, making it part of the United Kingdom. After 1800, Ireland had no government of its own but was ruled from the Houses of Parliament in Westminster. The famine was a powerful example of how Ireland's interests were not served by the government in England.

Daniel O'Connell (1775–1847) was a national hero at the start of the potato famine. He was a Member of Parliament who had fought for equal rights for Catholics, which resulted in the Catholic Emancipation Act of 1829.

To fight against the union of Ireland with Great Britain, O'Connell formed the Repeal Association in 1840 and held huge meetings (known as "Monster Meetings"), where he spoke against the Act of Union, arguing that Irish problems could only be solved by an Irish government. In 1842 a newspaper, the *Nation*, was founded by supporters of O'Connell's ideas. In no time at all, it became immensely popular. It printed articles on Irish history and culture, and campaigned for a self-governing Ireland. The men who created the paper, among them Gavan Duffy, John Mitchel and Thomas Meagher, became known as the Young Irelanders.

Daniel O'Connell died in 1847, at the height of the potato famine. The Young Irelanders, who had already broken away from the Repeal Association, formed the Irish Confederation and continued to campaign for repeal.

*

In 1848, another Irish hero and one of the leading members of the Confederation, **William Smith O'Brien**, attempted to start a rebellion, along with Thomas Meagher and other Young Irelanders, which was set to begin in and around Tipperary. Thousands of peasant people rallied and were raring to fight along with their heroes. Unfortunately, the willing crowds were totally unprepared, weak from starvation and without arms. The Young Irelanders were eventually arrested by British soldiers, tried for high treason, found guilty and transported to Van Diemen's Land. Irish resentment of British rule continued.

Many "repealers" fled or escaped from Ireland during or after the potato famine, along with the many people who emigrated to escape starvation – roughly two million Irish people emigrated between 1845 and 1855, mostly to the United States and Canada. Landlords, charities and relief committees would often pay the fare of destitute tenants, because it was cheaper than keeping someone in a workhouse for more than six months. Conditions on the emigrant ships were appalling, and thousands died during the long voyage over the Atlantic ocean. Still, the Irish communities that did manage to establish themselves in North America were fiercely loyal to their mother country and many continued to campaign for Irish independence.

Timeline of Ireland up to and including the 1800s

The history of Ireland and its relationship with England, is a long and complex one. This timeline includes a few dates which cover the years preceding the great Irish Potato Famine of 1845 to 1849 and the immediate years beyond it.

1760 Secret societies, whose members were known as Whiteboys, become an active and rebellious force, dispensing a rough and ready justice, mainly against landlords and rent collectors. Most of their operations take place by night.

1762 First execution of Whiteboys.

1778 and **1792** The Penal Laws which had prevented Catholics from owning, leasing or inheriting land are repealed.

1793 Catholics are given the right to vote for the first time in Irish history.

1796–1798 United Irishmen plot rebellion. Secret societies are springing up everywhere.

1798 Arrests and death of United Irishmen. Battle of Vinegar Hill.

1800 Act of Union creates United Kingdom of Great Britain and Ireland. Ireland is now governed from Westminster. The secret societies, such as the "Ribbonmen" – by now becoming the more generic term for these societies – grow ever more active throughout the first half of the century – they try to protect the interests of the poor by dispensing rough justice against the landowners.

1803 Robert Emmet leads a rebellion against British rule. It is crushed and Emmet is hanged.

1823 Daniel O'Connell founds the Catholic Association.

1829 Catholic Emancipation Act grants equal rights to Irish Catholics, who can now become Members of Parliament. O'Connell takes his seat in Westminster.

1831 National schools started.

1834 First Irish railway is built, from Dublin to Kingstown.

1840 O'Connell's Repeal Association is founded, which aims to end the Union with Britain.

1842 The *Nation* newspaper is founded.

1843 O'Connell's Monster Meetings preaching the need to repeal are held around the country. The largest one, at Tara, is attended by a quarter of a million people. The next one, due to be held at Clontarf, is banned. A week later O'Connell is charged and found guilty of conspiracy. He is imprisoned.

1844 The verdict of conspiracy against O'Connell is reversed by the House of Lords. O'Connell is released.

1845 About a third of the potato crop is destroyed by blight – this is the beginning of the Irish Potato Famine – the Great Hunger – which continues until 1849.

1847 Death of Daniel O'Connell in Italy. Soup-kitchen Act provides food for starving people.

1848 William Smith O'Brien leads the Young Ireland rebellion – it fails and Smith O'Brien, along with many of the leading Young Ireland figures, is arrested, found guilty of high treason and transported.

1858 Irish Republican Brotherhood (IRB) is formed by James Stephens.

1867 Rebellion by the IRB fails.

1870 Land Act gives some rights to evicted tenants. Home Rule was seen by many as the first step in the process of Ireland taking control of its own fate.

1873 The Home Rule League, which argues for Ireland controlling her own internal affairs, is founded by Isaac Butt.

Picture acknowledgements

P 177   **(top)** Sir Robert Peel, Popperfoto

P 177   **(bottom)** Pat Brennan's Cabin in *Pictorial Times*, Mary Evans Picture Library

P178   Daniel O'Connell, engraving by J Lewis, Mary Evans Picture Library

P 179   A peasant contemplates the poor potato crop, Mary Evans Picture Library

P 180   **(top)** Evicted tenants, painting by Frederick Goodall, Mary Evans Picture Library

P 180   **(bottom)** Distributing clothing to the poor at Kilrush, *Illustrated London News*, Mary Evans Picture Library

P 181   Homes of evicted tenants put to the torch at Glenleigh, Amedee Forestier in *Illustrated London News*, Mary Evans Picture Library

P 182   Evicted peasant and his family, Mary Evans Picture Library

Sir Robert Peel was the British Prime Minister at the time of the Potato Famine.

This illustration shows potatoes stored on a platform in the roof of a dwelling. Poor families would also have shared their home with the few animals they owned.

Daniel O'Connell formed the Repeal Association in 1840 in an attempt to end the Act of Union with Britain.

A painting from the time of the famine shows a peasant looking at the blighted potato crop.

An evicted family huddle by their padlocked cottage. Landlords would often burn properties to the ground and even dig up the foundations in order to prevent evicted families from getting any kind of shelter.

Newspapers printed many pictures such as this one during the years of the famine. This shows clothing being distributed to the poor.

Evictions continued for many years, as this newspaper illustration from 1887 shows.

An evicted tenant and his family.

Experience history first-hand with My Story –
a series of vividly imagined accounts of life in the past.

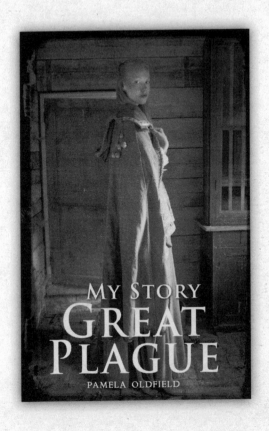

MY STORY
GREAT
PLAGUE
PAMELA OLDFIELD

MY STORY
MILL GIRL
SUE REID

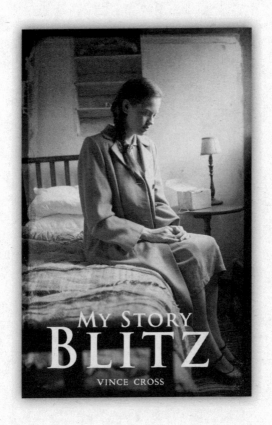

My Story
BLITZ

VINCE CROSS

MY STORY

TITANIC

ELLEN EMERSON WHITE

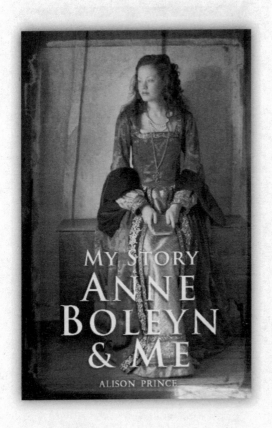

My Story

ANNE
BOLEYN
& ME

ALISON PRINCE

MY STORY
POMPEII

SUE REID

often?). But for all their real jeopardy, the spirit of the scene is at bottom deliciously comic (those striped shirts, for instance, with similarity underneath). It's one of Bowen's distinctive achievements, this fusion of comedy with raw emotional intensity. The writer sees through the scene to its funniness because she is not like Eva at all, of course, not stumbling in the dark of impressions – she's superbly capable of the higher-order reasoning, the 'putting things together' that a novel has to represent. Nonetheless, in Bowen's so-sophisticated writing, the forces of ignorance and appetite seem to operate almost as principles of vitality – her cleverness and scepticism redeemed by the blundering passions she represents, her writing touching earth through inhabiting them.

The whole manner of *Eva Trout* embodies strikingly this play in imagination between the writer's particular interpreting intelligence and her sensual openness to dreaming other people, other possible lives. Bowen's style is distinctive in all her writing – those prickly sentences, resisting conventional word order, and those descriptions straining conventional expectation, to capture perception newly and precisely. But *Eva Trout* has its own very particular style-world, and takes the distinctiveness to new levels. The leaps between the precise realisation through details and Bowen's explicitly authorial comments are more extravagant, less absorbed in the 'now' of the story; it's as if she's become, late in her career, ever more indifferent to concealing the authorial manipulations behind the writing, or keener to bring the processes of invention out into the open. The point of view is never restricted to the protagonists: often, the eye might as well belong to a film camera, and the perception to an intelligence behind the camera, impersonally noticing. When Constantine confronts Eva in her Broadstairs house he 'unhooded his eyes at Eva and levered his torso into the upright. Instantly, his attitude had about it something judicial and puritanical. She was addressed by the Bench.' That vision of the Bench doesn't belong – not consciously, anyway – to either of of how she was made. How can we not enjoy her sensual pleasure in her own cleverness, displayed to a class full of girls: 'Her dark suit might have been the habit of an Order. Erect against a window of tossing branches she stood moveless, but for the occasional gesture of hand to forehead – then, the bringing of the fingertips to the brain seemed to complete an electric circuit'.

Also, it's a measure of Iseult's distinction that she chooses unhappy, peculiar Eva, with her hidden reserves of feeling, to exercise her fascination on. She is less interested in impressing the other girls so much more superficially attractive, with their uniform 'clean hair, smelling of the school shampoo, oblong wristwatches, Connemara pullovers and a habit of humming [that] seemed to be universal. The pullovers seldom came off... when they did, under them were striped shirts, all of them tailored to the same pattern. And under the shirts? – again, similarity'. Later, as the plot unrolls, Iseult is so thoroughly paid back for everything that was unsound in her beginning with Eva – she loses, though it's not all Eva's fault exactly, her husband, innocence, even giftedness (when she tries to write a novel, it's born dead) – that any judgement against her seems ungenerously insistent, beside the facts of her fate. Judgement in the novel is dispersed, opaque, perhaps not ours to dispense. (Bowen writes that in a novel the '"moral light" has not, actually, a moral source; it is moral according to the strength of its power of revelation')[4].

This early school passage between Iseult and Eva (which is in fact a flashback in the novel's narrative) contains the seeds of so much that's going to go wrong as the relationship between them sours; one reads with trepidation as these two follow the marsh-lights of attraction, devotion, influence – going in too fast and too deep, Iseult taking on too lightly the burden of Eva's neglect and her needs (haven't 'brilliant teachers' done that all too

[4] *The Mulberry Tree*, p.44

But how can Eva believe in that thinly explanatory logic, after what she's been daily witness to – her father's histrionic, tormenting relationship with his male lover, the instability of relations and fortunes and happiness – and after how she's lived, apart from other children, isolated by her wealth and in perpetual transit, cared for by paid uncaring strangers? Her response to Iseult's offer, though, isn't repudiation. Naturally enough – because no one else, it's touchingly plain, has ever taken the trouble to wonder what this odd girl thinks at all – it's love, which 'like a great moth circled her bed, then settled'. In place of logic, Eva is overwhelmingly and disastrously open to feeling: 'she was kept amazed and awake by joy'. In a scene a little later, when Eva tries to talk to Miss Smith – really talk, through the worshipful words of a George Herbert poem she's learned in order to please the teacher who showed it to her ('But that my darkness may touch thine'), Iseult cheaply sidesteps into class-room tactics, cheating the moment's authentic emotional content: 'You see how pure language can be? Not more than two syllables – are there? – in any word?'

Are we supposed, then, to find Iseult disingenuous, manipulative, in adopting gawky, unpopular Eva as her worshipper? Well, she is, to some extent. Iseult must know how she dazzles Eva (literally, at the opening of the scene, when Eva steps off the path in wet bright spring sunlight, to let her teacher pass), and she must be basking in this adoration somewhat, using it to draw Eva close, magnetise her. Brilliance requires some adoring body to bear witness to it. (Later, Iseult's brilliance tarnishes, from an absence of admirers.) But the novel's judgement is always complex, never closes (not even on Eva's father Willy, not even on his wicked lover Constantine, Eva's guardian after Willy's death). Poor Iseult's manipulative vanity, enjoying her power over the girl, feels in its way as innocent at this point as Eva's abjection. 'About Iseult Smith, up to the time she encountered Eva', Bowen writes, meaning it, '…there was something of Nature before the Fall.' She is simply fulfilling herself, in terms spoken – overwhelms explanation. One of the things we learn about Eva early on is that when she was at school she needed help with her speech – or at least Iseult Smith, her teacher, thought so. (Bowen herself had a lifelong slight stammer – part of her attraction, her friends report.) But is there really any problem? Isn't it just that Eva's apprehension operates as the novel's does, through an intense openness to impressions which makes her own experience opaque to her, bewildering? Her speech is consequently abrupt and clumsy, the difficulties of true communication aren't smoothed over. Iseult wants to help her out of bewilderment; she wants Eva to learn to surmount her impression of the strangeness of things. ('Anywhere would seem strange to me that did not [seem strange].' Eva says.) In the place of strangeness, Iseult offers a higher-order explanatory logic, out of that day-lit sane aspiration of which the school is the temple, and she – brilliant, beautiful young teacher – is priestess and votary, 'in a state of grace, of illumined innocence, that went with the realisation of her powers'.

"...I *should* like you to think, though. You have thoughts, I know, and sometimes they're rather startling, but they don't connect yet" [Iseult said to Eva].

"Are they startling?" asked the gratified owner.

"They startle you, don't they? – But try joining things together: this, then that, then the other. That's thinking; at least, that's beginning to think."

Eva fitted her knuckles together. She frowned down at them. "Then, what?"

"Then you go on."

"Till when?"

"Till you've arrived at something. Or found something out, or shed light on something. Or come to some conclusion, rightly or wrongly. And then what? – then you begin again."

"Why, however?" Eva asked, not unreasonably.

move temporarily into a fantastically dilapidated villa in Broadstairs, further up the Kentish coast; for Bowen, in a characteristic reversal of the cliché, English seaside towns are carnival, unsound, stimulating places, where anything crazy might happen. Eva herself – oversized, inept and fabulously wealthy – is at a loss in life, something like a child dropped in at the deep end of adult entanglements and tragedies, given all the facts but no adult power to assemble them into a coherent narrative. This motif, of a blundering innocent causing havoc, tearing into the web of fictions by which the rest manage to live, is a recurrent motif in Bowen's fiction (there are the adolescents Portia in *The Death of the Heart* and Jane in *The World of Love*, there's odd Valeria in the short story 'Her Table Spread' – and any number of hyper-aware but ill-informed children).

It doesn't take too much ingenuity to trace the motif back to its beginnings in those crises in Bowen's childhood, the 'tensions and mysteries', 'chaotic shoutings' of her father's illness, and her mother's death.[2] After that death, Bowen writes, 'I could not remember her, think of her, speak of her or suffer to hear her spoken of.'[3] The survivors of disaster in her fiction aren't voluble, their disasters don't make them ask for anyone's pity. They have been afforded a glimpse – which sets them apart, and makes them dangerous – of the way things really are. Nothing might be all right, things might not work out for the best. Accident might at any moment overturn the best-laid plans, best-founded happiness. Chance is lordly, Bowen writes in her novel *The Little Girls*. 'Chance is God, choice is man.'

Bowen's writing isn't explanatory, never offers to sew neatly together the succession of accidents which make up any story. Her method is to work through a sequence of sensually realised scenes, whose sum of material content – weather, place, sky, furniture, the protagonists' physical selves, the words

2 *The Mulberry Tree,* p. 270.
3 *The Mulberry Tree,* p.290.

Introduction

Eva Trout was Elizabeth Bowen's last novel, published in the UK in 1969; she wrote it in her sixties, in the years after she moved to live in Hythe, in Kent – a place full of significance in her history. She and her mother had left Ireland when Elizabeth was seven years old, in flight from her father's mental illness, and they had made their home eventually in Hythe; her mother died there, from cancer, when Elizabeth was thirteen. Bowen placed the beginning of her writer's curiosity at that moment of unsettling translation, out of familiar blue-mountained Ireland into a Kent of seaside towns and bald chalk downs and the 'gigantic musical' of its past. Displaced as a child, she learned to see the strange under the surface of what appeared most ordinary. 'Submerged, the mythology of this "other" land could be felt at work in the ways, manners and views of its people, round me... with a blend of characteristic guile and uncharacteristic patience, I took note... after all, one of the main activities of the novelist'.[1] Displacement fostered her interest – like an anthropologist's – in places and people, and in the effects of places on people. She was always drawn to the differences between lives, rather than the things they had in common.

Something of the quirky, distinctive atmosphere of *Eva Trout* seems to come out of the renewal of Bowen's relationship with Hythe, scene of her writerly origins. She has her heroine Eva

---

[1] Ed. Lee, Hermione: *The Mulberry Tree, Writings of Elizabeth Bowen,* Vintage, London, 1999, p. 277.

CONTENTS

TO
CHARLES RITCHIE

Published by Vintage 1999

9 10 8

General Advisory Editor: Hermione Lee

First published in Great Britain by Jonathan Cape 1969

Vintage
Random House, 20 Vauxhall Bridge Road,
London SW1V 2SA

www.vintage-classics.info

Addresses for companies within The Random House Group Limited
can be found at: www.randomhouse.co.uk/offices.htm

The Random House Group Limited Reg. No. 954009

A CIP catalogue record for this book
is available from the British Library

ISBN 9780099287742

The Random House Group Limited supports The Forest Stewardship
Council (FSC®), the leading international forest certification
organisation. Our books carrying the FSC label are printed on FSC®
certified paper. FSC is the only forest certification scheme endorsed
by the leading environmental organisations, including Greenpeace.
Our paper procurement policy can be found at:
www.randomhouse.co.uk/environment

Printed and bound in Great Britain by
CPI Group (UK) Ltd, Croydon, CR0 4YY

ELIZABETH BOWEN

Eva Trout

or Changing Scenes

WITH AN INTRODUCTION BY
Tessa Hadley

VINTAGE BOOKS
London

ALSO BY ELIZABETH BOWEN

EVA TROUT

Elizabeth Bowen was born in Dublin in 1899, the only child of an Irish lawyer and land-owner. She travelled a great deal, dividing most of her time between London and Bowen's Court, the family house in County Cork which she inherited. Her first book, a collection of short stories, *Encounters*, was published in 1923. *The Hotel* (1926) was her first novel. She was awarded the CBE in 1948, and received honorary degrees from Trinity College, Dublin in 1949, and from Oxford University in 1956. The Royal Society of Literature made her a Companion of Literature in 1965. Elizabeth Bowen died in 1973.